D1545078

BOOKS BY

Clément Richer

TI-COYO AND HIS SHARK (1951)

SON OF TI-COYO (1954)

THESE ARE BORZOI BOOKS

PUBLISHED IN NEW YORK BY ALFRED A. KNOPF

SON OF TI-COYO

TRANSLATED FROM THE FRENCH BY

Gerard Hopkins

SON OF

OF

TI-COYO

CLÉMENT RICHER

New York : Alfred · A · Knopf : 1954

L. C. catalog card number: 54-7200

THIS IS A BORZOI BOOK,
PUBLISHED BY ALFRED A. KNOPF, INC.

FIRST AMERICAN EDITION

SON OF TI-COYO

CHAPTER I

EIGHT YEARS after the eruption of Mount Pelée there was no visible change in the desolation of St. Pierre de la Martinique.

The Americans had offered to erect in less than a year, on the mass of rubble and ruins, a new, modern, and model city of the kind they know so well how to build, as witness their sensational achievements at Colón and Panama. This miracle was to cost thirty millions. But the Government had protested loudly. Thirty millions was a fabulous sum, and it could be put to far more urgent, and desirable, purposes.

Many former ministers had been living in Paris, and even out of it, to whom, now that they were dead, no statues had been set up. Famous generals by the dozen were turning in their graves because they had not yet been able to clamber onto metal horses—preferably of bronze—in the middle of public squares, or at the corners of the avenues that bore their names—and all because the necessary funds had been lacking. Neither group of claimants —the defunct ministers and the late generals—could wait any longer. Thus it came about that the ruined city had to possess itself in patience—which it had long grown used to doing.

Besides, the Government had it in mind to set about rebuilding St. Pierre, some time, at a figure ten times less than the Americans were to charge for doing precisely the same thing.

The Americans gave way with a good grace. They asked nothing better than to see a friendly nation spared the expenditure of so much money—thirty million gold francs. They were reluctant to cause Lafayette the slightest pain.

Whereupon the Government made its first gift to

the shattered city. This took the form of something of the very first importance, something the need of which had been cruelly felt. And so it came about that the thousands of corpses buried beneath the rubble witnessed the arrival in their city (still filled with ashes) of a statue—the one thing in the world they most longed for—a statue of gray stone representing a woman with a gloomy face—very suitable in the circumstances—lying on her stomach, supported on her elbows, and trying in vain to rise.

That was fifty years ago, and she has not risen yet.

Nor has St. Pierre.

Then the Government turned its attention to other things (it had more than enough troubles), and the people now flooding back into St. Pierre took it upon themselves to erect, without any semblance of order or preliminary planning a host of miserable wooden shanties of every size and shape, which, wherever the opportunity offered, supported themselves against such scraps of blackened walls as the burning breath of the volcano had neglected to lay low. So successful were they in their endeavors that it was not long before the ancient city took on the appearance of a concentration camp for displaced persons.

From high above the town, Mount Pelée observed all this coming and going with interest. As was only natural, he had an idea at the back of his mind, but it was too soon to confide in anybody, and meanwhile the volcano gazed benevolently down on the newcomers in their huddle of hutments. Now that his anger was abated, his old familiars had returned. The lizards lay warming themselves on his denuded slopes, or scuttled up and down, as of old. Once more the wild woodland kids scaled his vertiginous peaks, above which great birds of prey hovered on outspread wings. Now that the trees had started to grow again around his feet, and the flowers to bloom before turning into sweet-tasting fruit, the birds, the bees, and the other insects could no longer resist his charms, but fluttered and buzzed all over the place, humming and chirping with joy. Even the snakes, which had made off when the eruption threatened, and, in their haste to be gone, had invaded the most frequented streets of the town, squirming about the feet of passers-by without striking—a most unusual thing with them—returned, once the danger was past, to settle down in the undergrowth that they had known since childhood.

Not many people, however, in this new St. Pierre remembered Cocoyo and his humble beginnings, and the hunchback now enjoyed the consideration and respect which are infallibly the lot of those who are possessed of a fortune and a reputation for good behavior.

In his luxurious home, surrounded by his family, Cocoyo lived a model existence. He scarcely ever ventured into the town, for he was far too busy keeping an eye on the men who worked his plantation to find time for loitering about the streets.

As for Ti-Coyo, he was completely happy so long as he could paddle his canoe, accompanied by the shark, and was rarely to be seen in St. Pierre. Dora, on the other hand, whose household chores had increased in number, went every day to market, whence she returned laden with food—and gossip. Such time as Cocoyo could spare from bullying the men whom he employed to weed the sugar-cane on his plantation, he devoted entirely to his grandson, whom he spoiled abominably, even when the child sucked his thumb or forgot himself in his cradle.

In honor of the sea, to which he owed his wealth, the hunchback had a long time ago painted his house on the outskirts of St. Pierre in bright-colored stripes. In memory of the first guinea that Ti-Coyo, with the shark's help, had picked up from the sea-bed, he gave to the boy the name of Guinéo.

Since the volcano had been at pains to dispatch elsewhere—far from this planet—all who might have been tempted to fasten insulting nicknames on the child, as they had done on his grandfather and father before him, Guinéo he was, and Guinéo he remained.

He was a charming infant, and well brought up (Lucie saw to that). The hunchback doted on him even more than did the others, though no child born into this world had ever caused his family more desperate anxiety.

The trouble, as they well knew, was that no power on earth could stop a Martinique boy from plunging into the sea whenever the opportunity offered, and it was obvious that a day would inevitably come when Guinéo and the shark would find themselves face to face in the salt sea waves. No matter how carefully the child was watched over, nothing, once he had grown a bit, could keep him from carrying out his intention of splashing about in the sea. All Cocoyo's cunning, and Ti-Coyo's too, was powerless to prevent that.

Although Cocoyo was careful never to allude to

this agonizing possibility, he was in a continual state of apprehension at the thought of a meeting that must, he knew, come about eventually between the shark and his grandson. The prospect filled his sleep with nightmares.

As to sacrificing the one to the other—the shark to the child—that would have been tantamount to suggesting that Ti-Coyo should let himself be cut open to have his heart torn out. Naturally enough, no one would so much as consider the alternative— the simplest and by far the most practical—of sacrificing the child to the shark.

The real, the only, the wisest solution, however, was to kill the shark in order to save the child, as everyone was secretly aware, and would have felt tempted openly to advocate had they not all known that Ti-coyo would as like as not have dug his knife into the first person who dared so much as to suggest such a course in his hearing.

That was how matters now stood. Meanwhile, Guinéo continued to grow, and the danger to increase with every inch he gained in height.

The only practical thing that Ti-Coyo had found to do—for he did not know which of the saints to engage on his behalf—was to sit with his baby in his arms close to the great tank in which the shark lay at his ease, at the far end of the path that led to the house of the late lamented white with five particles, just where it ran out on the little beach of fine sand where once he had waited breathlessly for Lucie to join him, so that he might take her far away and make her his wife. Perhaps, as a result of seeing the child on his lap for hour after hour and day after day, Manidou might later recognize him when they met in the sea, and so might be prevailed upon to spare him. Not that he didn't realize how ridiculous such an idea was, but what else could he do?

When Manidou saw Ti-Coyo arrive at the tank, he raised himself slightly in the water, retaining his position with an almost imperceptible movement of his lateral fins, and hanging there motionless, while he fixed his jade-green eyes on the worried father and, incidentally, on the object he was holding in his arms.

Ti-Coyo drew comfort from the absurd and irrational hope that the shark might grow accustomed to the sight of his son and, in the long run, come to understand the nature of the bonds uniting father and child. Needless to say, any such hope was altogether baseless, as he very well knew.

He was also aware, from personal experience,

that the creature lacked the most elementary notions of family life—family being a word without meaning for the general run of sharks. Dora had once very nearly learned this to her cost.

Manidou, for his part, could not understand why Ti-Coyo should be delaying for so unconscionable a time before throwing into the tank the delicate and wriggling little morsel he was carrying—some new species of mussel, perhaps, with the shell removed, or a clam of unusual shape. Whatever it was, mussel, clam, or anything else, the shark was quite certain of one thing, that Guinéo was bound to be good to eat.

In spite of the hopes built up so obstinately by Ti-Coyo that the shark might turn out to be endowed with unusual gifts of understanding, the creature saw nothing in Guinéo but an appetizer that his friend was holding back with the intention of springing a happy surprise when the right moment should arrive. But he was beginning to find the time of waiting somewhat protracted. He gazed at Ti-Coyo with a look of reproach, and at the delicacy—in other words, the child—with an expression of greed. That, at least, was how Ti-Coyo interpreted the shark's concentrated stare, and it made him intensely miserable.

"This is my son!" he cried to the monster in accents of despair, holding the child at arm's length above the tank. "This is my son! My son! My son! . . . Take a good look at him! . . . He's my own flesh and blood!"

The shark quite naturally failed to understand what was being said to him, and misunderstood the meaning of the gesture, thinking, in perfect good faith, that Ti-Coyo was preparing to drop the child into the tank. Consequently, he hastily raised his head above the surface so as to be ready to snap in mid-air at the falling object.

Great, therefore, was his disappointment when he saw Ti-Coyo walk away with Guinéo perched on his shoulder. Manidou felt, with some reason, that he had been cheated of a delicacy—what else could it be?—to which he was convinced that he had some sort of right—a delicacy that the other seemed to be constantly offering, only to withdraw the offer at the last moment. Such behavior, he thought, was lacking in loyalty. He was not used to being treated in that way, and lost himself in conjectures about the motives that could have induced his master to act so cruelly toward him. Surely, he had never done anything to deserve such scurvy treatment.

But a shark's patience is not easily exhausted, and

Manidou bided his time. A day would come, sooner or later, when the prize morsel that Ti-Coyo was so unaccountably keeping to himself would find its way, whether it liked it or not, into his belly, where it would be thoroughly at home—at least for a short while.

CHAPTER II

SOMETHING—and it was beyond the shark's power of comprehension—took place just after Guinéo's fourth birthday.

Ti-Coyo was still tirelessly, still despairingly, taking Guinéo every day to the tank in the hope that the shark might grow accustomed to the sight of him. The child ran about, and rolled on the grass and on the pebbles of the path, under the watchful eyes of Ti-Coyo, who never let him out of his sight.

14

Children are careless—and clumsy, too—and an accident is the matter of a moment.

But it so happened that a day came when the shark caught himself examining with a new sort of fixity—with new eyes—and with a sudden access of interest what he had grown accustomed to regard until that moment as a shellfish, or, anyhow, as good to eat. Suddenly the urchin reminded him of something, recalled to his mind an incident of the past— what it was he did not know—and the creature racked his brains in an effort to think what it could be.

Guinéo's appearance, the expression of his face, his every gesture, and even the inflections of his childish voice caused very old memories to rise to the surface of the shark's mind—memories of another child—they were alike as two peas—who, long ago, had kept him imprisoned in a different sort of tank—or had it been a lake?—on the slope of a mountain with its feet in the sea.

The creature rolled over heavily. His eyes were fixed on Guinéo, who was standing between his father's knees, and slowly a series of pictures formed in his great gray head, vague pictures that grew clearer as the child splashed about under his nose.

It was thus, and not otherwise, that a different child, the very image of this one, had crawled through the grass at the edge of a little lake on the mountainside. How could he be sure that this was not the same child, who, after all this time, had come back? *That* one had furnished him with the chance of many a succulent feast in the days when he dived in so ridiculous a way after little glittering objects lying at the bottom of the sea. The same boy had helped him to escape from a steel cage when he, Manidou, had been no more than a young, inexperienced shark without a thought in his head.

Manidou changed his position in the tank so as to keep an eye on Guinéo, who had moved away in pursuit of a dragonfly fluttering near by. The fin-bearer felt something very like nostalgia. Not many things can touch a shark's feelings. Nevertheless, Manidou was conscious of spiritual unease, a sort of dragging at his heart, as he watched the boy on the path, for something like this had happened to him years and years before, when, after escaping from his steel cage, he had lost sight of just such another child—it couldn't really be the same one—who had been very dear to him.

A woman (he had been within an ace of swallowing her some time later) had given him fish, but he hadn't felt like eating—not before he had seen Ti-Coyo in the courtyard between the mango trees, when he had jumped ashore to meet the child about whom he had been feeling so worried.

But all that had happened a very long time ago, before the mountain had caught fire and the sea had risen from its bed, carrying on its back all those succulent morsels—the bodies of men and women smelling of leather, caught up from the streets of the ruined city—which had turned him into the fattest, the longest, the heaviest, of all the sharks in the whole of the Caribbean archipelago.

Of these things did Manidou dream at the bottom of his tank as he watched Guinéo running to and fro on the path, and his mind was full of what had happened in the past.

As time passed and Guinéo grew bigger, the boy became an ever pressing subject of preoccupation for Manidou, and the cause of cruel uncertainty.

Nothing in his appearance, nothing in his expression, showed that he was paying him any particular attention, for sharks are by nature reticent. All the same, day after day he watched the boy playing near the tank—and he could scarcely believe his eyes.

There were moments when he asked himself whether Guinéo was really Guinéo, or whether Guinéo was not, in fact, Ti-Coyo in person. The shark became the victim of a terrible perplexity, and was inclined to believe that a trick was being played on him. Someone, he felt sure, must be twisting his tail, must be indulging in a bad joke.

On the other hand, mightn't he be suffering from hallucinations? Increasing age, he had heard, does sometimes bring troubles of that kind. He might, after all, be growing old, his eyes might be failing, for there was no doubting the fact that, in the glaring sunlight which drenched the path, he now found it impossible to tell Guinéo and Ti-Coyo apart.

Manidou regretted bitterly that it was not customary for sharks to consult an oculist and have their eyes examined. Beyond any doubt, a good pair of spectacles—on condition, naturally, that the rims were not made of tortoise-shell—would have helped him to see his way more clearly in this affair. Perhaps a set of carefully chosen lenses might have enabled him to understand how two Ti-Coyos could come to exist simultaneously in time and space.

Till now he had never felt it necessary to give to philosophers the amount of attention they deserve.

He had never read Descartes—Ti-Coyo had been too scatterbrained to recommend such studies to him. All the same, his instinct, and his long and fruitful shark-experience, led him to deny the possibility, the reality, of so strange a doubling of personalities—at least in the world as he knew it.

On the other hand, there was Guinéo before his very eyes, and so puzzling was his resemblance to Ti-Coyo—his gait, his look, even his way of turning cartwheels on the path, just as Ti-Coyo had done on the grass beside the little mountain lake—that unless he, Manidou, had become hopelessly short-sighted—or decrepit—there could no longer be any doubt either that Guinéo was Ti-Coyo, or Ti-Coyo Guinéo, which came to the same thing and did nothing to simplify the agonizing problem that he was trying in vain to understand.

Whatever the explanation might be, the very idea of snapping his great jaws on Guinéo, should the occasion arise, had become distinctly unpleasant, even repugnant, to him, greedy though he was for fresh, human food.

He had a feeling that swallowing Guinéo—if ever he had the chance, for Guinéo usually kept out of his reach—would be like swallowing Ti-Coyo at the same time. Such a thought was intolerable to him, and even the possibility made him shudder. He felt much as a man might do at the prospect of stabbing his own father.

Faced by the alternative of devouring Guinéo or devouring Ti-Coyo—he no longer knew where he was with the two of them—he felt himself confronted by something odious and sacrilegious as well, something on which he would not let his mind dwell.

Nobody can take lightly the idea of committing parricide.

Gradually Manidou abandoned any attempt to fight against the warm feelings he had for the boy—feelings in which greediness played no part, and the plumpness of Guinéo's little body had ceased to count. No longer was there any question of the shark's looking on Guinéo as a shellfish, and still less as a delicious dainty. He could not help feeling for Guinéo the same affection that he had for Ti-Coyo—could not help giving to one the tenderness he felt for the other—and that for the reason that he could no longer be sure which was which.

It was possible—the shark no longer knew what to believe—that Ti-Coyo was gifted with the power of going backward in time and assuming at will the outward form of his own past childhood. Manidou had heard tell of such things—but they had never happened in his own day, nor in the world he knew.

Everything is possible, he said to himself, rubbing his eyes with one of his lateral fins, and there is no knowing what might happen to a fool of a shark who has let himself get into such a bad state that he sees double!

In this way did Manidou tease his brains as he rolled from side to side in his tank, glancing the while out of the corner of his eye at Guinéo playing among the pebbles.

And so it came about that when at last the boy was able to articulate, more or less distinctly, three syllables in succession, and to call the shark correctly by his name: "Ma—ni—dou," in the very same voice that Ti-Coyo had used in the old days when uttering the same word, the shark leaped in his tank and turned over three times, trembling from tail to fins, much to the surprise of Ti-Coyo, who, naturally enough, could not guess the reason for so great a display of emotion.

From that moment, and that day, the shark gave up altogether any attempt to apply his mind to the problem, or to resist the impulse, or the feeling of affection, which drew him to the boy.

He now abandoned, once and for all, any hope he

might have had of understanding how Ti-Coyo could be Guinéo, or vice versa. Such a puzzle, he saw clearly, was beyond the competence and understanding of any shark to unravel. He was up against a miracle, and he must accept it without argument, just as he had had, for instance, to accept that the sky and the sea were both blue, though they were not of the same substance, and never, at any moment, met, as young sharks thought they did.

So Ti-Coyo made off, leading Guinéo by the hand, and the shark let himself sink down till his belly was lying on the sand at the bottom of his tank.

From now on, Manidou knew, beyond the shadow of a doubt, that if ever he met the boy in the sea, he must inevitably fling himself into his arms.

CHAPTER III

GUINÉO was eagerly looking forward to the day when he should be three years old, for he knew that he would be taught to swim as soon as he had reached that advanced age. All the children of Martinique feel this same excitement, and are never really happy until they have learned to move about in the water, and under it as well, when their lawful, and as a rule important, occasions call them there.

Guinéo, therefore, hurried on with his growing, and in next to no time was in a position to reckon three whole years from the moment of his birth. He began to wonder how Ti-Coyo would initiate him into a science so thrilling—the science of natation, on which he counted to derive much delight.

But on the very morning of that memorable day he was to experience the first disappointment of his life. Ti-Coyo, instead of going with him along the path that led to the beach—and the sea—as he had expected and hoped for three times three hundred and sixty five or six days, calmly branched off in the direction of the Roxelane, into which he threw him without more ado, as he might have thrown a common or garden stone, and left him to get out as best he could, in a spot where the river was quite deep enough to accommodate several three-year-old brats put end to end.

As soon as Guinéo rose to the surface, without a breath in his body, he naturally opened his mouth wide with the intention of calling for help to his father, who was standing on the bank, apparently thinking about something else. But then he swallowed half the contents of the river—or so it seemed to him—before sinking again suddenly, and much against his will.

When he emerged for the second time, Ti-Coyo was still there in the same place on the bank, whistling between his teeth, and he now had with him a number of black-hearted people—out for a morning walk—who guffawed loudly, probably because they remembered how, at the same age, they had made the same brilliant start in life—and in the water.

Guinéo realized then—his little brain working with the speed of a turbo-jet under the stress of the moment—that there was no help to be expected from any living creature. Instead, therefore, of opening his mouth to give vent to another cry, as he had done previously, he kept it firmly shut so as to prevent the remaining half of the river from getting into it.

He decided that he had drunk enough, and more than enough, for one day. He confined himself, therefore, to threshing about in the water with his diminutive limbs, for all the world like one of those tadpoles to which he bore, just then, so strong a resemblance, in a desperate effort to reach the bank.

But it was far less easy to do than, up to now, he had thought it would be, and he felt a strong conviction that he was going to die before the goal was gained. He failed to understand how there could be any water left in the river after all he had swallowed, and he expected to see the level of the Roxelane sink before his eyes.

Clearly, he would have to make several more descents to the bottom, though he felt a strong repugnance to exploring it any farther for the moment. Meanwhile he gulped down several bumpers of excellent water. After a number of attempts, however, much queaziness, and a conviction that the life was being squelched out of him, he did manage to keep at least his nose above the surface—though never for as long as he wished—until, at last, just as he had resigned himself to death, he felt the good solid sand under his feet.

He moved rather unsteadily through the grass, slumped down on his behind, and burst into sobs.

"You didn't do too badly," said Ti-Coyo as they were walking home, "but tomorrow you'll do better still."

Guinéo had so often begged to be taught to swim that he did not like to hang back now. Consequently, he did not dare do more than venture a timid diversion.

"Couldn't we wait a little while?" he suggested, his voice choked with sobs; "say until next week?"

"Not a hope! When one has started something,

one's got to go through with it; so we shall go back
to the river tomorrow morning, and the morning
after, and the morning after that, and so on, until
you feel as much at home in the water as the sh—as
I do," Ti-Coyo hurriedly amended the words, always careful not to refer to the shark's habits in his
son's presence.

Guinéo heaved a sigh—a deep sigh. He knew that
his father would be as good as his word, and that
nothing he could say would change by a jot or tittle
a decision of this kind. So he wiped the tears from
his face with the back of his hand and nestled his
head against his father's shoulder, feeling thoroughly miserable.

For some reason or other he was no longer quite
so keen about learning to swim as he had been.

In the course of the next few weeks and months
Ti-Coyo took Guinéo with unfailing regularity to
the Roxelane and stood on the bank, whence he
calmly and unfeelingly watched the boy's efforts
to master an element in which he would later have
to pass a considerable portion of his life. And so it
came about that, toward the end of the year,
Guinéo informed the hunchback, in an offhand sort
of way, that there were not many people in

Martinique, with the possible exception of Ti-Coyo, who could swim and dive as well as he could.

Cocoyo relayed this remark to Ti-Coyo, who laughed loudly when he heard it. All the same, he thought that the time had come to take certain precautions. When a child shows *that* degree of self-confidence, his parents soon begin to worry. The boy now spent most of his time playing about in the river, and Ti-Coyo, who had other things to do, had long since given up accompanying him on these expeditions.

On one occasion, when the hunchback had expressed some anxiety about his safety, the boy replied that he was now perfectly capable of making his own way to the beach, adding that he might be tempted, one of these days, to try his luck in the sea.

On hearing this, his grandfather uttered a cry of terror, and Ti-Coyo made it quite clear to the boy—accompanying his words with an evil grin, which Guinéo, who knew his own little world, was not slow in interpreting at its face value—what would happen to him should Guinéo take it into his head to go closer to the shore, and the sea, than was necessary. The latter of these two places, Ti-Coyo pointed out, was the private domain of Manidou, who would certainly not consent to share it with anyone, except perhaps with Ti-Coyo himself.

Guinéo listened attentively. To all appearances he was completely convinced. Still, as Ti-Coyo observed later, words are one thing, deeds another.

In order, therefore, to encourage the deed, and so give point to a sentence as full of wisdom as his had been, Ti-Coyo thought it well, when the boy's birthday came round, to give him an adorable little dog, with which Guinéo instantly fell in love.

The little dog ate out of his plate (when nobody was looking), slept in his bed (as soon as Lucie had tucked the boy up and gone away), and followed so faithfully at Guinéo's heels that after a very little while Guinéo could no more have done without him than the volcano could have done without its crater.

When it came to a question of swimming lessons, Guinéo behaved to his favorite, not unnaturally, just as his father had behaved to him. He was much surprised, however, after throwing the little dog as far out into the river as he could, to see him return calmly to the bank and conscientiously shake himself, without having gone through those processes of sinking suffocation, and sobbing which had marked Guinéo's progress after a precisely similar initiation.

The boy, who refused to admit (though it was, in fact, the strict truth) that the little dog was a good deal abler and cleverer than he was, found himself driven to the rather dishonest conclusion that his favorite must have learned to swim before becoming his property. No doubt his mother had taught him as soon as he was born.

All of which goes to show that Guinéo was a great hand at lying to himself, for Dora had already explained that the puppy's mother had died in giving birth to him and seven of his brothers, none of which resembled any of the others, probably because they had all had different fathers—though she said nothing about that. The child, she decided, had his whole life before him in which to learn about such subjects.

When the little dog had reached the age of six months, and Guinéo was quite certain that if it died, he would die too, Ti-Coyo took them both one day—the dog and the boy—to Manidou's tank at the far end of the path. Holding Guinéo's hand in his, and pressing it in the most affectionate manner possible—the boy had no idea what was to happen next—he propelled the little dog, with a sudden swing of his foot, straight into the tank, where the shark hastened to meet it, thus saving it a good half of its journey.

The little dog disappeared down the creature's gaping maw, in which the teeth had suddenly become erect and menacing. Guinéo uttered a loud cry and showed every intention of going to his dog's assistance. But Ti-Coyo's hand was firmly clenched on his, and all that happened was that the boy twisted his arm and suffered a good deal of pain in the process.

Manidou wriggled about in the tank in a delirium of joy, because if there is one thing in the world that sharks love above all else, it is dog's flesh—a peculiarity that they share with the Chinese.

This fact was familiar to Ti-Coyo, and that was why, six months earlier, when Guinéo had started to boast about being the best swimmer in the district, he had given him a dog, without informing him that it was destined, as soon as it had won Guinéo's affection, to end its short life in the shark's stomach.

Ti-Coyo had not liked doing this, for he was a great deal fonder of animals than of people. But his purpose had been to show the boy, by giving him an object lesson more eloquent than any words could have been, exactly what Manidou was capable of, and to breed in him a salutary fear of the fin-bearer. It was the only way in which he could prevent his son from swimming out into the harbor of St. Pierre—and becoming acquainted with the inside of the shark's throat.

Guinéo sobbed until he thought his heart would break into a thousand pieces, and it was then that Ti-Coyo had solemnly explained that if ever he found himself face to face with Manidou, he would stand about as much chance of getting safely away as the dog had done.

"And now," he said in conclusion, *"you know,"* with which words he made off, feeling more or less easy in his mind, thus proving once again how little parents understand their children.

CHAPTER IV

Guinéo was now nearly seven years old, and behaving as though he were twenty years older.

He was scarcely ever seen in the house or running through the plantation, for he had far too much to do exploring the Roxelane up and down, and down and up, to devote much time to his family. He usually started off in the morning, came back at midday to eat, and then disappeared again until the evening.

"That grandson of mine has got his hands full," said the hunchback with a wink.

That was true enough. But if Cocoyo had been able to guess what the boy was doing, he would have jumped several feet into the air.

It was Dora, a month later, who started the hare. She took the hunchback aside. "Look you," she said, "there's a spirit loose in this house—some zombi for certain."

"I know," replied Cocoyo in high good humor; "it's me."

"It's no joking matter!" retorted Dora, whose face expressed anxiety. "For months and months now somebody's been taking money from my purse."

"But who could do a thing like that?" exclaimed Cocoyo, suddenly brought up short.

"How should I know? It must be a spirit. Who else could get into my room?"

The hunchback frowned, deep in thought. "How much money has been stolen?" he asked.

"Not much at any one time, but a little every day—I'm sure of that. For a long time I thought I must be mistaken, and didn't want to mention it, but now I know: I marked some of the coins."

"Hm," said the hunchback. "I bet it's one of the

plantation workers. Probably took the job so as to rob us. I'm going to get to the bottom of this."

For a whole week Cocoyo kept careful watch, but discovered nothing. When Sunday came, and they were just finishing their midday meal, he decided to take the others into his confidence.

"I noticed some similar petty thieving last year," said Ti-Coyo; "so I put my purse in a different place, and the thief gave up trying."

The hunchback was dumfounded. "And you didn't see fit to tell us?" He spoke so vehemently that the young man burst out laughing.

"Oh," he said, "I thought it was you doing a little thieving on the side."

Cocoyo was speechless with indignation, but he got really angry when Lucie confessed, rather hesitatingly, that she had been the victim of a similar theft some time before, and that she, too, had hit on the idea of hiding her purse. She had said nothing, because she had shared Ti-Coyo's notion about the identity of the thief.

"I said, didn't I," Dora intervened before the hunchback had time to set fire to the house and bury Ti-Coyo and Lucie in the ruins, "I said there was a spirit loose in the house."

Cocoyo gave a furious snort and shrugged his

shoulders. He had never dreamed that anyone in his domestic circle could have so good an opinion of him. Besides, he did not believe in spirits who stole money—especially when that money was a family affair, and when the business had been carried on under his own roof.

"It's certainly possible," he said with an absent-minded air, and then, becoming suddenly calm: "Yes, it's perfectly possible."

He gave a sidelong glance in Guinéo's direction. The boy was sitting beside him, eating away with a good appetite, and not paying any attention to what was being said.

The hunchback, still deep in thought, went off to take a walk in the plantation, his mind busy speculating about the laws of heredity. The appetite of which Guinéo had just given so remarkable a proof was causing Cocoyo considerable anxiety. Had it been merely a matter of rice cakes or chocolate creams, he would not have worried. But what had been on the boy's plate just now had been spinach, and he remembered how in the past, whenever spinach had been on the menu, Lucie and Dora had had to promise Guinéo everything under the sun in order to get him to eat it. This was why, a few moments later, without saying a word to anyone, he sought out the plantation foreman and asked him whether he was married, and whether he had any children. The man both was and had.

Cocoyo was prepared to give the foreman's son—the one who was twelve years old—a ten-franc piece if the lad would do as he was told. The foreman gave his word of honor that his son was obedience incarnate, and that if anyone gave him a ten-franc piece, there was nothing he would not do in return. Cocoyo then proceeded to explain in detail what it was he wanted, after which he walked away, nervously flicking his crop.

"I've found the thief," he announced three days later, when the family was assembled around the dining-room table. "He is here, in this very room, seated among us."

Lucie looked at Dora, who squinted at Ti-Coyo, who told the hunchback to explain what he meant.

"Oh," said Cocoyo with an air of detachment, "he's quite a small thief."

Guinéo began to squirm and quietly pushed his chair back, the better to make a getaway as soon as the moment came which he knew would not be long delayed.

Every eye was now fixed on the boy, who was sitting with his nose obstinately buried in his plate.

"But why the devil should he want to steal?" said Ti-Coyo, voicing his surprise.

"What's bred in the bone—" said the hunchback, cynically, quoting the proverb. "Also, he needs money to buy fish, though what he does with the fish when he's got it beats me. The foreman's son says he sees him every day buying from Robert Fil de Fer in the market and then making off without leaving a trace."

"Perhaps he resells it," suggested Dora, who boasted a Chinese in her family tree. "I come of a line of merchants," she reminded him in accents of pride.

In the Caribbean islands every Chinese sells something—no matter what—cheaper than no matter whom, and thus manages to grow rich. The mystery has never been cleared up. But Ti-Coyo refused to accept this solution. He, too, pushed his chair back and went across to where, in a corner, the leash belonging to the little dead dog was lying. Guinéo had been playing with it before they sat down to their meal. It was of plaited leather, and was apt to leave red marks on anyone's skin when it was used for punishment.

Cocoyo cleared his throat with embarrassment. "I'd done a little stealing before you were born, and you followed in my footsteps," he observed quietly to his son; "and don't you forget it."

"I know all about that," said Ti-Coyo impatiently, "but I never stole from my own people, nor you from yours. Besides, we both of us had an excuse, because we were poor and needed the money, which is not the case with the boy, and—"

The hunchback, confronted by so obvious an example of bad faith, was all agape. "In the days when you used to come to this plantation to steal the sugar-cane belonging to the white with five particles," he said in a voice heavy with reproach, "I had a chest full of gold at home. Lucie can bear witness to that."

Lucie looked down and blushed. She did not like memories of this kind to be trotted out before her son.

"Parents," continued the hunchback, for he wanted to spare his grandson a thrashing, "parents forget that they've been kids themselves." He spoke indulgently, without raising his voice, for he did not want to irritate his son, knowing how hotheaded he was. But Dora was less tactful.

"The one thing that a thief hates most," she said,

quoting a Martinique proverb, "is seeing another thief with a full sack on his shoulder."

This could only make matters worse, and Ti-Coyo shook his head impatiently. "What this boy needs," he said coldly, pointing to Guinéo, whose whole attention was concentrated on each jerk of the dog's leash in his father's hand, "is a good lesson, and that's what he's going to get right now."

But Guinéo had already jumped out of his chair, and had gone like the wind through the open door. Ti-Coyo was hard on his heels, with the family following at a respectful distance.

The boy turned to the right and went rushing down the path toward the sea. He was moving fast.

The hunchback was the first to notice Ti-Coyo standing stock-still in the middle of the path, as stiff as a post in an ox-pen. His face was livid, and covered with great drops of sweat, which he was making no attempt to wipe away. The boy was not to be seen.

Cocoyo's legs refused to carry him farther, and he stayed where he was, trembling from head to foot. His mouth was hanging open, but not a word could he utter.

A few steps behind him came Lucie, her face whiter than a bridal veil. She gave vent to a stifled groan, and collapsed senseless into the arms of Dora, who, for the first time in her life, was vainly trying to focus both eyes on a single object—the shark's tank.

The hunchback seemed to be seeing things through a mist. He could just make out Ti-Coyo walking toward the tank—very slowly, as though his every step would be the last. Then he leaned forward quickly, and straightened up again with a dripping object in his arms, whereupon Cocoyo, who could no longer trust his legs to carry the load of his two humps, collapsed on the front one and lay stretched across the path.

As soon as the child had been dried, rubbed with Eau de Cologne, smothered in kisses, and coaxed and wheedled in every possible way, the hunchback stood him in the middle of the dining-room table, just where the steaming soup-tureen was ordinarily put. Then, as soon as everyone was seated, as though for a meal, he said:

"Now tell us all about it; I really did think my last day had come."

His head still felt dizzy, and his legs were a bit unsteady. He might have reproached Ti-Coyo, but what good would that have done? He might have pointed out that never in the whole course of his existence had Ti-Coyo received a beating, and that when, in the old days, it had been a question of correcting him for some piece of naughtiness, Co-coyo, instead of giving him a thrashing, had been satisfied to tell him a story, like the one about the casuarina trees.

But about all this he said nothing. His stomach felt as though it had turned over, but the boy was safe. All he wanted to know was how the miracle had happened. But Guinéo sat for a while saying nothing, and scratching his curly pate with an expression of considerable embarrassment. Then he sniffed once or twice, noticed that Lucie, who had taught him the use of a handkerchief, was frowning, felt in all his pockets for the one he was supposed to carry, and, quite naturally, failed to find it.

He coughed, not in order to clear his throat, but because he had noticed that that was what the hunchback always did when he had something important to say. Guinéo was fully conscious that all eyes were turned upon him.

As soon, Guinéo explained very calmly, sitting, with his legs crossed, in the middle of the table, as soon as he felt certain that he was a more skillful and more experienced swimmer than his father, he made up his mind, after due reflection, to establish friendly relations with a creature who was strong enough to swallow a six-month-old dog in full flight. He could not reach the tank by the path, because Ti-Coyo had given him strict injunctions not to do so, and because Ti-Coyo (here Guinéo squinted sideways at his father) was always, for no apparent reason, brandishing the leash of the deceased puppy. The best thing to do was to approach the tank from the sea, and that was what he had decided to do whenever he could be sure that the grille was closed and the shark securely confined. Guinéo had no wish to risk a premature meeting with so formidable a personage. He knew—Dora having told him so—that the best way of gaining the monster's favor was by feeding him fresh fish every day. That, she had said, was what Ti-Coyo had been in the habit of doing, as a result of which he was now on terms of intimate friendship with the shark.

"I had to tell him something," muttered Dora, uneasily, "just to get him off to sleep."

Ti-Coyo here broke silence to observe that in those far-away days Manidou had been no more than a baby shark of scarcely sixty pounds' weight, but that now this same Manidou would turn the scales at not less than six tons.

Guinéo moved his shoulders in a faint—and disrespectful—shrug. He failed to see that the weight and age of the shark had anything to do with the question, or could make any difference. It was then, he went on, that the idea had come to him to get the necessary fish by stealing—

Dora cleared her throat loudly.

"It is a weakness that runs in our family," remarked the hunchback ironically.

—By stealing, Guinéo proceeded, unperturbed, the money he needed from Ti-Coyo's pockets. It had been months before his father had noticed anything. When he finally did, he had said nothing, but had merely put his clothes somewhere else (Guinéo had never been able to find the key to the wardrobe where they were now hidden). Guinéo had been driven to making raids on Lucie's purse, and later, when she, too, had hidden her purse, on Dora's.

"I, it seems, was singled out for favored treatment," muttered the hunchback, from whom nothing had been stolen. "Am I to understand that I was being regarded with peculiar deference?"

Nothing of the kind, said Guinéo, and he proceeded to disillusion the hunchback, without mincing his words, giving his reasons clearly and without beating about the bush. They were simply that he had reckoned on Cocoyo's low cunning to discover the theft, seeing that he was forever counting and re-counting the smallest coins in his purse. As he said this, Guinéo made a face, which expressed better than any words his disgust at such sordid avarice.

The hunchback scowled. "Go on!" he said curtly.

Guinéo felt all through his pockets again in search of a handkerchief, but was no more successful this time than he had been before (Lucie said that he lost, on an average, at least a dozen every week). Then he decided to venture on another sniff, glancing furtively at his mother to see what effect this new proof of his lamentable upbringing would have upon her.

In order to get fresh fish he had had recourse to Robert Fil de Fer, a fisherman of the district who was so long and so thin that he really was like nothing on earth so much as a piece of wire—hence his name.

He, too, however, was a consummate thief, said Guinéo bitterly, and had made him pay a stiff price per pound. It had been no good protesting, because there was a danger that his provider—who knew only too well that a boy of his age couldn't spend that amount of money every day—might take it into his head to noise the news abroad. Some day he would make Robert Fil de Fer pay, and pay dearly, for the way he had behaved, declared Guinéo, who, like all the members of his family, had a long memory in such matters.

Ti-Coyo nodded his approval. No doubt about it, Guinéo was a true son of his, blood of his blood, who never forgot a grievance and was all on fire to avenge it.

Later, he had stolen—

"What, again!" broke in Lucie, scandalized, but the hunchback merely shrugged his shoulders with indulgent tolerance.

—stolen a basket from the larder.

"So it was you, was it!" exclaimed Dora.

Guinéo admitted that it had been, and described how he had filled the basket with fish, shut the lid, and hung the handle round his neck. In this way he had left his hands free for the swim across the harbor of St. Pierre, and had reached the path where Manidou's tank was situated.

There he had opened the basket and thrown

the fish one by one to the shark, at the same time addressing to him the kind words which, according to Dora, Ti-Coyo had used in the old days.

Dora looked contrite and hung her head. Ti-Coyo gave her a far from complimentary stare. He had always been very careful to say nothing before the boy about his past relations with Manidou, and now it turned out that Dora had been busy, behind his back, making up for lost time. Was nobody to be trusted?

"You are very naughty, Manidou," Guinéo had said to the shark, who was engaged in snapping up the fish as they fell one after another in his tank; "my father says so, and I know he's right, because you ate my poor Cric" (that had been the dog's name), "who never did you any harm. . . . What about this for a piece of prize mackerel?" he broke off to observe. "But I'm not a little dog," he went on; "I'm Guinéo. Get a hold of this eel. Robert Fil de Fer says it weighs three pounds!"

Manidou caught the eel, as he had been told to do, and the boy continued with his monologue, telling the shark more things, probably, than the creature bothered to listen to; after which he swam back again across the harbor, this time in the reverse direction, with the empty basket slung round his neck, dressed on the beach, where he had hidden his clothes under a rock, and returned home.

He had gone on in this way for more than a year, or not much less. Like Ti-Coyo long ago, Guinéo did things thoroughly. Then, one day, what anyone could have seen would happen did happen. Just as he was preparing to throw a large mullet to the shark, his foot slipped and he tumbled into the tank.

"Ah!" said the hunchback, with a sharp intake of breath. "And what happened then?"

"Nothing at all," said Guinéo calmly. "I shut my eyes as I fell, because I remembered how the little dog had been gobbled up, and I shut my mouth, too, because I didn't forget that my father had kept the leash of that same little dog and might be tempted to use it if he found out where I was." It was Guinéo's opinion that a man should preserve his dignity.

"To hell with the leash! And to hell with dignity!" Cocoyo bellowed with an oath. "What did the shark do?"

The shark had not so much as stirred a fin. Perhaps, though that seemed unlikely, he had not seen the boy fall. Perhaps his somewhat sluggish brain could not distinguish between the boy before

him and another boy, whom Guinéo was as like as
two raindrops and who once upon a time had
brought him fish in precisely the same way.

Whatever the reason, Guinéo could not spend
the rest of his life there; so after a moment, as soon
as he realized that nothing was happening, he tried
to scramble out of the tank. But his legs were too
short, and all he could do was cling to Manidou's
broad back. The shark turned his head slightly,
because Guinéo was tickling him.

But he said nothing, though he did not much
like the sensation, and the boy, once he was out of
the tank, threw him all the fish still lying in the
bottom of the basket. Then he took his departure,
after first expressing his thanks to the fin-bearer
in the politest possible terms, though, if the truth
be told, his voice was rather unsteady.

Those round the table heaved a profound sigh
(the hunchback mopped his forehead, which was
damp with sweat), and Guinéo, noticing the effect
produced by his story on his audience, seized the
opportunity to sniff unrebuked.

That night, before going to sleep, he had taken
time to do a little thinking and reached the conclusion that if the monster, who was usually prepared to gulp down anything—or anybody—had not

so much as nipped his little finger, though he had been completely at his mercy, the reason must be that Manidou now entertained for him, as formerly he had entertained for Ti-Coyo, whose son Guinéo, after all, was, feelings of affection. Undoubtedly the shark loved him as he had loved Ti-Coyo.

"Yes," Guinéo had said to himself that night, into his lace-trimmed pillow, for it was time for him to go to sleep and he could barely keep his eyes open, "yes, he does love me, and I must pay him another visit in the tank. After all, what can happen?" He snuggled down under the blankets. "I'll push the fish into his mouth and so save him the trouble of having to catch them as he does when I throw them from a distance. Cric used to love it when I put lumps of sugar in his mouth. I wonder whether Manidou's fond of sugar, because, if he is, I can steal some from the kitchen."

"He can't get away from that word 'steal,'" moaned Lucie in despair.

"Your father," remarked the hunchback spitefully, "once said—long ago, and he's dead now— that we were a family of thieves."

Lucie hung her head, and Ti-Coyo tapped with his fingers on the table, which was his way of telling the hunchback to be quiet, and showing his annoyance when the other went too far.

On the very next day, as good as his word, Guinéo, with the basket round his neck, slipped into the tank under the shark's very nose, holding in his hand a mackerel, which the monster swallowed after first turning on his side, it being a peculiarity of sharks that their mouths are under their chins.

When not a fish was left in the basket, Guinéo gave him lumps of sugar which he had stolen that morning from the kitchen, from under Dora's nose, and these, too, the creature swallowed, probably out of politeness, and because he did not want to hurt the boy's feelings. As a matter of fact, if Guinéo had offered them, he would have swallowed a petticoat or a cavalry saber, for sharks are catholic in their tastes where food is concerned, and besides do not suffer from indigestion.

Guinéo acquired the habit of joining the finbearer in his tank, and telling him all sorts of things —whatever, in fact, happened to be in his mind at the moment—until one day, when he was out swimming in the harbor, he came face to face with Manidou, who had been let out earlier than usual.

The shark spent a few moments swimming round and round Guinéo, but, being engaged on urgent business some miles away, made as though to move off, leaving his companion behind.

But the boy would not put up with such treatment. In terms of authority he called the shark back and told him that, wherever he was going, he had got to take him too. Manidou slowly retraced his steps. He felt extremely embarrassed. Nothing was farther from his wishes than to disoblige the boy or to be guilty of boorishness toward him. On the other hand, he was in a tearing hurry to keep an appointment he had with several shoals of bonito in the Dominica Canal. Much perplexed, therefore, he made a few circles round Guinéo, who, with a lack of understanding natural to his age, laid hold of one of his lateral fins and so got himself towed for more than two hours from end to end of the Dominica Canal, which is the last place in the world where anyone would think of swimming for pleasure.

The boy was so light and the shark so heavy that the latter had to turn his head from time to time to make sure that Guinéo was still hanging from his fin. The shark would have been loath to abandon the boy, who would have been quite unable to make his way back unaided to St. Pierre.

Besides, Guinéo was too easy a prey, and too delicious a morsel, for any other shark to resist, and Manidou, who felt responsible at this moment, would not have left him there in mid-ocean for anything in the world. He was by no means the only one of his species—though none were comparable to him in weight and size—to haunt that locality, and a brat like Guinéo would be quickly swallowed.

But such fears were baseless, for it never so much as occurred to Guinéo to loosen his hold on the fin. He wasn't far from believing that the shark had arranged for that extremely convenient appendage to be placed exactly where it was for his benefit, and he clung on, without weakening, through the whole of the journey—Manidou was engaged on something more than a saunter, but a boy placed as Guinéo was, on the shark's back, could easily make such a mistake.

It was a very wonderful, though very dizzy, trip, an experience, indeed, such as nobody has ever dared to imagine, even in dreams. The only objection was that Guinéo could not clap his hands for joy, for had he tried to indulge in any such ill-timed manifestation of that kind, it is probable that matters would not have turned out so well for him. But nothing untoward occurred.

So successful, indeed, was the trip that he got into the habit of waiting for the shark every day in the harbor about the time that Ti-Coyo raised the grille of the tank, and, once firmly attached to the fin—always the same one—of letting himself be taken far out to sea, according to Manidou's whim —and appetite.

On the return journey the shark would stay for a while floating and resting in the water at some distance from the town, and Guinéo would do the same, stretched out on his back close to the fin-bearer. Every now and again he would pat the shark's back, calling him his *"gros doudou,"* in much the same way as he had patted the head of his little dog, calling him by the same name.

When, by chance, strangers turned up on the scene—a fishing boat or even a cargo vessel—the two friends would loaf off, one towing the other, though it was always the same one who did the towing. The fishermen would naturally have felt obliged to go to the rescue of an eight-year-old boy if they had spotted him in the sea so far from St. Pierre. Matters would have been still worse if they had noticed in his proximity the fin of so impressive-looking a shark as Manidou. Guinéo dared not think what the reactions of a boatload of fishermen might have been to a sight so unusual. Consequently, he was at great pains to put a considerable distance between himself and other humans and boats. The shark's society—and not the companionship of other boys of his own age—was all that he wanted.

When Manidou decided that it was time to go home, he set a course for the tank, and Guinéo would accompany him as far as the grille, much as a lover might take a pretty girl to her own front door after a dance—the only difference being that Guinéo was still too young to aspire to the status of lover, and that the shark bore no resemblance to a pretty girl.

"And what happened then?" asked Ti-Coyo, breathless with astonishment, for he had never dreamed—except once, during a storm, the memory of which was far from pleasant—of so singular a mode of locomotion as consisted in hanging on to a shark's fin and being dragged through the ocean.

"That's all," answered Guinéo, with modest reticence, once more hunting through his pockets with no hope of finding a handkerchief. "Manidou and me go out every day now, and if I happen to be late—when Mother keeps me here with her awful reading and writing lessons—he waits for me out in the harbor until I turn up."

Cocoyo swallowed hard, and there was a long silence around the table. Finally the hunchback shook his hump with an air of pride and, pointing with a hand that shook with emotion at his grandson, who was now sitting cross-legged where the tureen should have been, he said in a voice full of conviction: "Look! That's my grandson, my son's son! Blood always tells!" Cocoyo excelled in introducing into the conversation the various sayings that he kept in reserve with this intention.

All the others showed their approval noisily—all, that is, except Lucie, who was descended from crusaders and saw no reason why the hunchback should be proud of the nameless—and inferior—blood that flowed in his veins.

But Guinéo had not told all.

He had refrained from relating how, on one occasion, when he had been lying on his back out in the harbor, in company with the shark, enjoying the movement of the rollers, a smack had noiselessly appeared and taken them by surprise.

The expression on the face of the fisherman in

the bark, and the direction of his gaze, had left
little doubt of his state of mind, and Guinéo had
found no difficulty in realizing that it was a matter
of the utmost urgency to shut the man's mouth before he had time to spread about the town news
of what he had seen—a shark and a boy rocked by
the same wave.

So Guinéo, without losing his head, or any time,
had at once begun to act as though he were drowning—thrashing about in the sea, and fighting for
breath—and doing it so well that the fisherman, not
knowing what to think, had decided to go to his
assistance. At the precise moment, however, when
the man leaned forward and stretched out an arm
to seize the boy and pull him out of the water,
the shark, suddenly surfacing at Guinéo's side, managed to snap the man's arms off at the elbow, so
that he tumbled overboard.

The operation had been very efficiently carried
out—without noise, without witnesses, and without
risk—except for the fisherman, whose boat drifted
slowly onto the beach. He himself was never seen
again.

On two other occasions Guinéo, though lacking
the excuse that he had been surprised by a boat
appearing out of nowhere, had played the benev-

olent role of lure for the shark, who lay hidden between his legs. It goes without saying that Manidou thoroughly relished this new strategy which the boy had discovered, though not intentionally, to provide him with new prey—those sturdy fishermen of St. Pierre for whom he had always shown a predilection and whom Ti-Coyo in the old days had furnished him in abundance.

No doubt about it, the shark was a happy fish— he congratulated himself on the turn of events— now he knew that the son was following in his father's footsteps, though there was still a deal of confusion in the shark's mind, for he could never be certain which was which, or whether the one was not the other, and so on.

It was, in truth, the most amusing occupation in the world to splash about in the sea calling for help, and then suddenly diving—just as the fisherman was leaning from his boat to drag him from the water—so as to leave the field free for the shark, who was ready to look after the rest of the business.

This impromptu little game was played to perfection by each of the two actors—Guinéo and the shark. Even the supers (the fishermen who were cast for the supporting roles) performed with much naturalness and sincerity, entering with a will into the skin of the part—always the same—which Guinéo and the shark wanted to see them play.

To topple overboard a man standing in his own boat, with his arms just snapped off at the elbows, was both exercise and entertainment for the shark, as well as the occasion for a good meal at a cheap rate.

But Cocoyo, who was endlessly indulgent toward Guinéo, was hard put to it to find a really adequate excuse for such behavior in a boy of eight.

CHAPTER V

THE SHARK, when he was not in his tank, spent his time in the society of Guinéo, tacking up and down in the harbor, whence he watched with ever increasing interest the flow of immigrants, which grew daily more substantial, into the old city.

Each new shanty that went up among the ruins brought to the shark a fresh access of moral satisfaction, for he knew that human beings would settle there who, sooner or later, would succumb to the temptation of taking a bathe in the warm, calm sea that stretched before their windows.

The folk of Martinique have a passion for salt water, and this brought much happiness to Manidou. He rejoiced to see the new arrivals turning up in carts loaded with luggage and children, and drawn by fine horses, which those same children would have to lead down to the water, there to scrub and bathe them. Both men and horses must bathe if they want to keep well, and the more of them there were to take baths, and the oftener they did it, the happier Manidou would feel on their behalf.

None of these people—or horses, for that matter—had heard, naturally enough, of Ti-Coyo, and still less of his shark—a fact that Manidou considered a further good mark in their favor.

It was Dora, a short while later, who brought the news back from market one morning that a shark, larger than anyone could have imagined, and unbelievably brazen-faced, had leaped out of the sea and felled, with one blow of its tail, hardly three yards from shore, a magnificent mare that had been taking a bath under the watchful eye of a young boy whose parents had come to settle in St. Pierre a week earlier.

This boy, instead of sensibly returning home, had felt obliged to stay jumping about on the sand and shouting for help. The shark, which had lost no time in gulping down the mare, had returned, no doubt attracted by the noise the boy was making, had nabbed him in his turn on the shore, and sent him to join the mare in his stomach.

"A horse's place is in its stable," announced Ti-Coyo sententiously.

"And the boy must have been extraordinarily lacking in prudence," said the hunchback, in support of his son's statement, hopping about the drawing-room and twirling his gold-handled crop.

"Hm!" remarked Dora, with an evil squint; "according to the fishermen, three of them have not returned home recently, and they're saying now that the shark is responsible for so long an absence."

"A man may have all sorts of reasons for not going home," replied the hunchback, "and it's ridiculous to blame sharks for disappearances of that kind."

"Nevertheless," said Dora, "that is what these two men are doing."

"What men?" asked Cocoyo, who was completely out of touch with what was happening in the town, for he never went there any more.

"South Africans," explained Dora, "or that's what

they call themselves. They're talking about ridding the harbor of this murderous creature."

Cocoyo pricked up his ears, and Ti-Coyo frowned. He did not like his shark to be threatened, and the insult seemed to him doubly outrageous coming from foreigners.

"I'm going straight to St. Pierre," declared the hunchback bluntly after turning the matter over in his mind. "I want to find out what all this is about, and to know who these people are and what they propose to do."

He had himself driven through the town, where, by gossiping with a number of people—no one could gossip more skillfully—he soon found out that the two men of whom Dora had spoken were brothers, who had arrived a few days before from Pretoria, which, as everyone knows, is the enlightened capital of a still more enlightened country.

They were called Ben and Bill Gardner, and they did not like half-castes, which, after all, they were entitled to do. Still, in view of the fact that every human being born in Martinique is more or less of the same racial type, it was difficult to see why they had come to St. Pierre, where there is scarcely anybody else.

Cocoyo, much enlightened by what he had heard,

next limped down to the beach, where he knew that most of the fishermen would be occupied, at that time of the day, in mending their nets and calking their boats.

A few of them were St. Pierre men who had been absent from the town on the day of the eruption and had since returned. But the greater number were newcomers from all four corners of the island. Cocoyo took it upon himself to remind the first, and inform the others, that there had always existed in the harbor of St. Pierre a shark who was nothing less than an incarnation of the Spirit of the Sea. He took the trouble to explain, with the addition of hair-raising details, how that shark had once escaped from a wire net, the lid of which— listen! ponder! and tremble!—could be opened *only from the outside,* and how Nat the Mulatto, whose idea the net was, had perished miserably a short while afterwards.

He spoke so eloquently that he soon had his audience shaking and listening to him with their eyes starting from their heads.

"That's the truth," agreed the St. Pierre fishermen in chorus. "That is perfectly true."

"I remember it all," piped up another, with a head of gray hair and not much brain inside it.

"Oh, don't I remember it! . . . There was another who disappeared, too, and a third who had helped in making the wire net. Have you forgot?" he added, nudging his neighbor with his elbow.

The neighbor had arrived the day before from the commune of Macouba and had never heard of the affair before. Nevertheless, he hurriedly and with a deal of self-importance asserted that the whole story was still clear in his mind, and this he did in order to make the others believe that he was a native citizen of the old town. Now, as murmurs of terror and amazement rose all about him, he swelled with pride.

The hunchback took his departure, leaving the men to think things over and discuss what they had heard. He knew that their first concern when they got home that evening would be to pass on the story, with additional embellishments of their own, and that their wives wouldn't be able to stay still for a single moment until they had handed on to all their friends at market a very much magnified version of it.

And so it came about that the next time the South African spoke about killing the shark, he found the fisherfolk more than usually reticent. When he found out the reason for their lack of enthusiasm, he made no bones about mocking, loudly and at length, what he called "the gross superstition of these natives, and their incredible stupidity."

The fishermen disliked this kind of talk intensely. When, however, the South African mentioned that he was going to send home for one of the large-bore guns that are used for elephant-hunting and for shattering the armored hides of crocodiles, he was listened to more attentively, and the knives, already pulled half out of their sheaths, were noiselessly pushed back again.

With a weapon like that, he would quickly purge the waters of the harbor, once for all, of the marauding shark, and he rather thought, he added, that the "Spirit of the Sea," about whom he had heard till he was sick of the subject, would think twice before taking a chance with a man born in Pretoria.

The fishermen gave every sign of being impressed, not so much by the mention of the speaker's birthplace as by his description of a gun that was capable of pulverizing an elephant or a rhinoceros in a few seconds. The fact that none of them had ever set eyes upon these redoubtable pachyderms, except in pictures, did much to increase their respect for the South African's weapon.

There was not much difficulty in getting them to promise that as soon as Bill Gardner should have got his gun from home—in a fortnight at the longest—they would search the waters of the harbor for the shark. He and his brother were making a pleasure trip to Martinique and had no intention of leaving it for a month or two.

After all, it would be a good thing—an unhoped-for blessing—if the South African turned out to be as good as his word and really did succeed in killing the shark. In any case, the attempt would be well worth making, said the fishermen, who only half believed that such an exploit was within the power of mortal men to achieve, especially after everything that Cocoyo had told them on this subject. Long experience—a tradition dating back several centuries—had taught them that no human being, whether born in Pretoria or elsewhere, had much to gain by entering into direct conflict with the Spirit of the Sea, which had always made a quick end of those who dared openly defy him, as witness what, according to the hunchback, had happened to Nat the Mulatto and to several others.

To such comments Bill Gardner, hitting the nail

on the head, replied that Nat the Mulatto, as his name showed, had been nothing but half Negro, whereas he himself was an unadulterated South African white. This consideration could not but have a marked influence on his dealings with the Spirit of the Sea.

There might be a good deal of truth in this contention, after all, and if the fishermen felt some surprise at such an astonishing and, to the ears of men of Martinique, new argument, they did not show it. Thereupon the South African burst out laughing, with a self-satisfied look, and his listeners went home with something fresh to think about.

Meanwhile Cocoyo, whose ears were everywhere at once, lost no time about finding out what was in the wind respecting Bill Gardner's projects and the nature of the promises made by him to the fishermen. His first care was without delay to pass on to his son all that he had heard, and Ti-Coyo looked far from pleased.

A man who has taken as much trouble as Ti-Coyo had done to lay the foundations of a prosperous career, and has spent so many years in building up a fortune, does not see that fortune threatened at its source without feeling upset. Not that money meant anything to him. He would not have minded becoming twice as poor as he once had been, if only he could be left in possession of his shark—and the sea. Cocoyo and Dora, however, did not altogether share his feelings on the subject.

"It's a serious matter," declared the hunchback, shaking all over with anxiety. "What the devil are we going to do about it?"

Needless to say, Ti-Coyo was not going to stand idly by while somebody, no matter who, took a shot point-blank at his shark. So he replied calmly that he could see nothing to do but cut off the South African's head some dark night.

"There's no moon just now," he remarked, for he was a young man who believed that there was nothing like speed in affairs of this nature.

"Don't be in a hurry, my boy, don't be in a hurry," said the hunchback. "Cutting off people's heads is nothing, and it's all the easier when it's a question of such a fool, but—"

"How do you know he is a fool?" put in Dora, who was present at this council of war. "You don't know, and besides—he's got a magic gun."

Cocoyo had his answer pat: "A man of sense would have kept his intentions to himself, and his magic gun too, until the shark was safely out of the way. But this chap tells everybody everything he's thinking about."

"That's true," agreed Dora. "He must be a mad-man."

"A fool," the hunchback corrected her severely.

"It's the same thing," Dora conceded with a good grace. "But my son's going to cut his head off."

"No doubt, no doubt. But the police will want to know how the man came to die. Have you thought about that?" Cocoyo went on, turning to his son.

"My knife doesn't leave clues," was the reply, short and sharp.

The hunchback, however, did not altogether like the idea, and he managed to get Ti-Coyo to undertake that nothing should be done until another day had passed, though the young man gave his word with a bad grace, being anxious to get the whole business over with. Manidou was so deeply embedded in his heart and in his life that Ti-Coyo felt as though the danger was hanging over his own head no less than over the shark's.

"What's the point in waiting?" he asked irritably.

"Just twenty-four hours to think things over—is that too much to ask? Have a little patience, my boy. It's just as well to sleep on things like this— and remember, *I* wasn't born in Pretoria."

"Where *were* you born?" inquired Dora maliciously, for she was well aware that the hunchback knew nothing about his birth or his origins.

Cocoyo's only reply was to shrug his shoulders with annoyance. He didn't, at the moment, feel much like laughing. Besides, he had got an idea at the back of his mind—an idea suggested by something he had heard that the South African was planning.

CHAPTER VI

It is a little difficult to agree with Mount Pelée's estimate of its own importance. Nevertheless, its dizzy and serrated crest, its sharp, denuded flanks, did give to the volcano that savage beauty and primitive grandeur which usually appeal to those whose feelings are susceptible to the appeal of noble heights and dramatic scenery.

Just such a one was Bill Gardner.

He never grew tired of looking out of his open

72

window at the mountain's imposing mass whenever the sun, according to the time of day, hung
the volcano with pink scarves and ribbons of shot
mauve, or, just before nightfall, swathed it in a
mantle of scarlet. At those times it seemed to quiver
with pride and self-satisfaction, leaning against the
sky like some great savage beast propped against
a background of blue granite. The sight filled Bill
Gardner with impatience. He felt that he could not
rest until he had scaled the marvelous peak and set
his feet upon its summit.

But when he spoke of his intention to other
people, their faces assumed a grave expression. The
volcano, they said, was full of traps for the un-
wary, and only a madman would venture on its
slopes without an experienced guide—someone like
old Madeira, for instance. One climber had disappeared in this or that year, another in that or
this, without leaving a trace, and that, too, long before the eruption. Mount Pelée did not surrender
the bodies of its victims.

But Bill Gardner was better informed. He was a
man who knew what he wanted, and he wanted
this particular thing very much indeed—and without delay. Those with whom he discussed the proj-
ect were careful, therefore, not to press their ob-

jections too strongly. He was determined to undertake the ascent the very next day, should the weather be fine. He didn't, he said, need any bastard nigger at his heels—nor anyone else for that matter—to scramble up the sides of a mountain which, after all, had nothing in common with the Himalayas, or even Mont Blanc, which he had climbed successfully five years earlier when on a trip to Europe.

And so next morning before dawn he set off on the road to the mountain, with coils of rope, ice-axes, spiked sticks, and a mass of paraphernalia which made those whom he passed look at him with incredulous eyes. For they knew that Mount Pelée was a bare four thousand feet or so in height.

He negotiated the lower bastions, and very soon found himself among crevasses from which rose noxious fumes and rumbling noises, which set the near-by rocks aquiver. A little farther on, liquid lava stirred with a sort of deathlike movement, while at times the ground all but opened under his feet with a most unpleasant cracking noise.

The mountain was full, too, of strange sounds for which he found it hard to account.

No doubt the whole place was inhabited by whole colonies of woodland goats who had returned there after being driven away by the eruption. But to Bill Gardner the cries they uttered did not seem altogether natural. The fact is that these wild young goats now and then called him by his name, while the stones that they dislodged each time they leaped from rock to rock fell unpleasantly close to his feet. Besides, the spurs of basalt on which the kids stood, gracefully poised or pawing the ground, were much too far away to make it possible for the stones dislodged by the hoofs of these charming creatures to reach the spot where the South African was negotiating the painful ascent with the aid of his spiked sticks.

More than once already he had stopped to listen, and to scratch his head with an air of perplexity when there reached him the three syllables of his name: "Bill—Gard—ner!"—each clearly articulated, though amplified and, naturally, distorted by the deceptive echoes of the savage gorges on every side of him. But he was the only living person there. Mount Pelée is not a public garden, and most people just out for a walk find somewhere else to go. To make sure that he really was alone, he now and then looked carefully about him. To be sure, the place was littered with rocks behind which a man might easily have hidden, but who could be interested in playing so dangerous a game? And what reason could he have?

Try though he might to drive them from his head, he could not help remembering the stories passed round by the fishermen and their wives about those spirits of the sea and the mountain who lured wanderers on with sounds and visions until they went out of their minds or became hopelessly lost. It was in just such a way that Nat the Mulatto had perished, if the fishermen could be believed. At the end of two hours of difficult climbing, Bill Gardner had lost much of his self-confidence.

He was several times tempted to turn back, but he had talked too much about this expedition. If he went back now to St. Pierre without having reached his goal, people would say "We told you so." He pressed on, therefore, though his heart was by now full of apprehension.

He did not, of course, share the absurd superstitions of the ridiculous natives. All the same, each time he heard his name pronounced from behind him—or sometimes from in front, or again just a little farther off—he sheered away, without admitting it to himself, and changed direction with a little involuntary shudder.

Sunlight drenched the mountain, filling the depths between the sharp ridges with shadows, which without any apparent reason kept on changing their position. Suddenly Bill Gardner stopped, trembling all over. A stone launched by heaven knew whom, and from heaven knew where, had struck him on the cheek.

In vain did he turn his head in every direction and carefully inspect the space around him. All he could see was a great vulture high above him, seemingly too much occupied with its own affairs to be throwing stones at a stranger's face.

Nevertheless, for the fifth time since he had started his climb, Bill Gardner found himself moving in a more southerly direction, and away from the line of approach he had set himself to follow. He could not help feeling—absurd though it was—that someone had put into his head the idea of trying to climb the southern escarpment instead of the northern one, which had seemed to him to offer the easiest approach, and from which he had been warned not to diverge. But whenever he turned south he heard his name spoken in mocking tones by some invisible goat with a human voice—if such a thing were possible—or was struck on the back or head by a stone.

If he told this story in Pretoria or Johannesburg, nobody would believe him, but it was true, right enough.

About noon, he debouched, breathless, onto a narrow platform that was blocked by a flat, gray slab of rock, on which he could have lain down for a rest had he not been in such a hurry to finish his climb and get clear of the mountain.

Something deep within himself, some mysterious instinct, warned him to work his way round the gray rock just as he was about to set foot on it. It was then that close behind him a voice suddenly shouted his name loud and clear: "Bill Gardner!"

The South African gave a violent start and swung round, but as he did so, he tripped against the gray rock and fell on it at full length. Before he could get to his feet, the rock toppled over to one side, and, with a loud cry, he shot off into space.

At that very moment, over the top of another rock—not behind him, as Bill Gardner had thought, but in front, for nothing is so deceptive as a mountain echo—Cocoyo's head came into view.

The hunchback had been keeping on the track of the South African from the first moment that the latter had set foot on the volcano, hiding behind crags, circling round and round the climber, lying flat in the shelter of rocks or in crevasses, for, as will be remembered, the hunchback was familiar with the locality and knew every nook and cranny of the mountain. Thus hiding, now on one side of his victim, now on another, he had managed, by dint of throwing stones, or mockingly calling his name, to keep the South African on the right road—the one that Cocoyo wanted him to take because it would lead him at length precisely to the large, flat, gray slab which, as the cunning hunchback knew well, had a way of suddenly tipping over as soon as anybody put his foot on it.

Very slowly it had resumed its normal position, and Cocoyo could not resist the temptation to utter a little titter when he saw, lying beside it, the coils of rope and the ice-axes with which Bill Gardner had been encumbered, just as they had rolled when he had fallen into the abyss.

"Really, a most regrettable accident," muttered the hunchback ferociously through clenched teeth.

Then he hopped nimbly over the slopes of Mount Pelée on his crooked legs. He was in a hurry to get home, for the long morning on the mountain had put an edge on his appetite.

. . .

"The man with the magic gun's got lost on the mountain!" Dora informed him next day. She had come back from the town and the market in a great state of excitement. "There's a search party out!"

"I hope they'll find him," replied Cocoyo unctuously.

Dora gave a little start and stared at her hunchbacked husband. "You hope they'll find him, do you?" she said slowly. "You hope he'll come back and shoot the shark?" Such a declaration from the hunchback's lips was so surprising, so unexpected, that she stood stock-still for three long minutes, squinting all about her. "Ah!" she said at length, recovering her breath.

There was no need for Cocoyo to say more. Dora knew now, without the shadow of a doubt, that Bill Gardner would never more return from the mountain.

"Your father *hopes*" (she deliberately stressed the word) "that they'll find the man with the magic gun who's got himself lost on the mountain," she said to Ti-Coyo when he came home, a little later, from the sea.

Like Dora somewhat earlier, Ti-Coyo raised his head and stared long at the hunchback, who was picking his teeth. "Ah!" he said at length in his turn, and drew a sharp breath. That was all.

The members of Cocoyo's family needed no more than a hint to understand one another.

CHAPTER VII

ALL THROUGH the following week a rescue party, led by old Madeira, who knew the mountain better than anybody else—with the exception, of course, of Cocoyo, who kept the extent of his knowledge to himself—tirelessly searched the northern slopes of the volcano, sounding every crevasse and peering under every rock. But they found nothing.

Madeira gave an impatient shrug when Ben Gardner, brother of the missing man, who took an

82

active part in the search, suggested that they should explore the southern slope as well.

"What's the point?" said the old fellow. "No one ever goes that way, and I myself saw your brother —saw him with my own eyes—setting off on the north slope."

"Maybe," replied Ben Gardner, with no great warmth; "but he may have changed his mind on the way and taken another direction. I want you to look round the other side, too."

So off started Madeira again, with Ben Gardner and the rest of the search party at his heels. They continued the search all that morning, and examined the southern slope. A little before noon they came on the gray slab and saw beside it the coils of rope and the spiked sticks that had slipped from Bill Gardner's hands when he fell.

"Bill can't be far off!" cried the South African, and made as though to go forward.

But the old guide caught him roughly round the waist and held him where he was until he grew calmer. "Now, don't you get excited," he said harshly to the South African, who released himself with a furious look. "I give the orders here, and I don't like the look of that rock."

The guide remained for a few moments studying

the gray slab with suspicious eyes. Then he glanced round him, as though looking for something. At last he found it.

It was a large lump of quartz which must have broken loose, as the result of some earth tremor, from a neighboring mass of rock. With the help of the rest of the party, Madeira dragged it down and let it fall on the slab.

"Look now," said the old half-caste to the South African, "how that slab tilted under the weight of that lump of quartz and sent it over the edge. That's the road your brother took, for sure. No point in your going the same way."

The members of the party stood rooted to the spot, unable to speak. Their eyes were wide with terror as they saw the great gray shelf of rock slowly resume its ordinary position, closing the abyss.

"No one ever comes this way," said the guide slowly, "so how did he reach this place if it wasn't the spirits of the mountain who pushed him here to stop him from meddling with the shark who is their emanation in the harbor of our town?"

The others, as with one voice, loudly expressed their agreement. How else was it possible to explain so strange an accident, and Bill Gardner's extraordinary behavior? There was no doubt about it in their minds; Madeira had merely put into words what each of them had been thinking from the beginning.

Ben Gardner said not a word, but bent down and collected one by one the various objects—the ice-axes and the rest—that had belonged to his brother and were now scattered all about the gray rock. Then, still silent, he followed the others, who had turned for home.

Not a soul in St. Pierre but shuddered with horror when news reached the town of the South African's disappearance and the circumstances surrounding it. For days and weeks nobody talked of anything else on the waterfront, at market, or in their homes. The general view was that the hunchback had been perfectly right, and that those who were so ill-advised as to threaten the shark inevitably came to a premature and very strange end. Even the skeptics could not but be struck by the unusual way in which the South African had met his end.

Cocoyo, however, for some reason that Dora could not make out, seemed to be uneasy in his mind.

"Why don't that fellow say something?" he muttered, pensively scratching his head.

"What fellow?" asked Dora, with a look of surprise.

"The brother of the one who got lost on the mountain," replied the hunchback with commendable tact.

"What do you want him to say?"

"Anything so long as it's something!" growled Cocoyo in an ill-tempered voice. "Just cast your mind back. His brother was always talking—talked so much that he died of it. But this one never says anything—not a word!"

"Is that what's bothering you?"

"That's just what it is," admitted the hunchback, whom Ben Gardner's silence was now preventing from exercising his usual care in supervising the plantation.

"Bah!" said Dora, who never saw beyond her nose. "Why should he say anything? Nothing he could say will bring his brother back from that hole you toppled him into."

The hunchback merely shook his head and set off down the road to the harbor, where he hobbled about, chatting with the seafaring folk who were gathered there. He wanted to know when the ship was due at Fort-de-France which would have Bill Gardner's magic gun on board, and fell into a fit of deep cogitation when he learned that it was expected in two days' time at latest.

When he returned home, there was still a preoccupied look on his face. He shut himself away in a little room adjoining his bedroom. There he kept, all neatly arranged, dried herbs and flowers, together with some roots and scraps of bark scraped from he alone knew which trees.

He carefully picked out a small, black, twisted root that looked something like a mandragora, and set it to boil in his famous pot with the two spouts. During the process he muttered a lot of unintelligible words, not in order to hasten the boiling, but to invoke the assistance and favor of certain "spirits" of whom he had knowledge. When the brew was ready he poured it into a bottle, which he corked with care and slipped into his pocket. He also pocketed a bottle of milk and a bowl of coarse earthenware. This done, he betook himself to the washhouse, which he had transformed into a carpenter's workshop, and there, with the help of some solid planks, set himself to construct a small box, in the lid of which he pierced a number of small holes. He waited until it was dark and then slipped out of the plantation and took the path that led to the southern slope of the mountain.

He went steadily on through a tangle of flowering creepers and dense brushwood which now covered miles and miles of ground under the bastions of the volcano, until he reached a spot where a magnificent forest of giant trees had stood before the eruption. After walking for another hour he came at last to a place carpeted with waving grasses and surrounded by high tree ferns and clumps of bamboo.

In the middle of this clearing, and well in view, he set the earthenware bowl, into which he poured the contents of the milk bottle. To this he added the liquid he had obtained by boiling the twisted root of heaven knew what plant, after first stirring it with a twig.

Then, with an agility with which no one would have credited so malformed a creature, he clambered into a young calabash that grew near by. He put his crooked legs round the trunk and, by clinging with his fingers to every small asperity in the rough bark, hoisted himself up until he reached a spot where two branches interlaced. Here he settled down as comfortably as he could and stayed motionless, gazing intently at the clearing, and listening to the night sounds.

Not one human being in sixty years had visited

this place into which the hunchback had deliberately ventured, for it was a well-known assembly point of the vipers, those snakes of Martinique whose boast it is that no one, after making their acquaintance, has ever lived for more than ten minutes with or without an injection of serum.

This spot was their favorite haunt, and not a man or woman could have been found in all St. Pierre willing to risk a visit to it, even in broad daylight (vipers hunt only at night), and even with the certainty of discovering one of those fabulous treasures which, in the old days, the buccaneers of Tortuga were said to have hidden secretly at the foot of Mount Pelée. Most of the buccaneers, it is true, had been, as a rule, massacred on their way back by the local Indians, who converted them into those roast joints and breaded cutlets of which they were fond, with the result that the treasure had remained, for the most part, where it had been buried under the vigilant eye and savage guardianship of the volcano, which brooded jealously over it, and had, in order to make it quite safe from possible marauders, hired the vipers, at enormous cost, to keep watch during the hours of darkness.

The wild animals, just as surely as the humans,

knew that these dreaded snakes haunted the spot, and those that lived in the undergrowth on the opposite side of the mountain were careful to give it a wide berth.

For a whole hour the hunchback kept watch from his branch without seeing a living thing—not even a rabbit, not even a mongoose, whose presence there might have been expected. He could hear frogs in the distance happily challenging one another from their different ponds, and the green grasshoppers shrilly exchanging news, while the night birds replied from bush to bush in melancholy tones. Nothing stirred in the clearing except the light, which moved furtively as the moon accomplished her unhurried journey between the peaks and above the shoulder of the mountain.

Half hidden by the dense leaves of the calabash, the hunchback gave a sudden start and held his breath when at last he saw, emerging from the undergrowth, and slithering through the grass, a snake, which stopped dead in the middle of the open space and raised itself slightly on its tail, at the same time making a faint hissing sound, after which it began to turn round and round, like a dancer executing some mysterious and beautiful ballet step, with the rays of the moon shining and glinting on its scales, which gave off a sheen as of precious metal.

"It's a female," thought the hunchback, "and a very pretty female too—and she's waiting for her lover."

He was not mistaken, for in next to no time a second snake appeared, though it was impossible to say from which direction it had come. The tip of its somewhat shorter tail was distended—a sure sign that it was of the stronger sex. It slowly approached the first, in front of which it came to a halt, twisting and wriggling in a ceremonial fashion. Coiled opposite each other, the two creatures swayed their triangular heads rhythmically from side to side, every now and then touching tongues, behavior that in other places would have been regarded as highly improper and a sure sign of bad upbringing, so certain is it that different animals have different customs and varying codes of intercourse.

Cocoyo had no doubt that the vipers were expressing, by this touching of tongues, what all lovers feel in the moonlight. He very soon noticed, however, that the female hissed angrily whenever her lover pressed her too tightly or showed signs of becoming too enterprising, and the hunchback smiled ironically. Cocoyo knew that the males of the species have two of what it is usual to have only one, and that, more wonderful still, they can use both at once, a gift for which many people envy them. But he knew, too—and the female snakes are certainly not ignorant of the fact—that these two organs are equipped with cruelly sharp spikes, which curve inwards like claws and so prevent the female from slipping out of the male embrace, for snakes lack arms with which to press the loved one to their breasts. Consequently, though the female snakes love to be courted, they are rather less eager to make husbands of creatures who carry sharp spikes in such a very awkward place.

Eventually, and without the male having obtained what he passionately wanted (how heartless women are!), the lovers moved side by side toward the bowl of milk, of which they had been perfectly well aware from the beginning, though they had been averse from showing it. They plunged their elegant heads into the bowl, and started to lap up the contents with a daintiness that Madame de Pompadour could not have equaled in her lifetime and might well have envied.

They remained at the bowl, looking at each

other and at the clearing around them, until, suddenly, the second to arrive—the male presumably—stretched himself out and lay motionless and soundless, while his companion took a good five minutes more to do the same, though she had imbibed just as much of the hunchback's drug as he had done. The sight led Cocoyo to reflect, in disillusioned mood, that women, generally speaking, have a greater power of resistance than men, though they never cease complaining of their weakness—and that, in any case, there are more widows in the world than widowers, as all statistics show.

At this point Cocoyo climbed slowly down his tree and, without taking the slightest precaution, approached the snakes, which he picked up quite fearlessly and stuffed into the box he had made for the purpose that same afternoon.

When Ti-Coyo went down at dawn next day to raise the grille of the big tank in order to release the shark, as he did every morning before setting off on his business, he found the hunchback waiting for him at the end of the path so as to beg him to do nothing of the sort.

"Let him fast today," said Cocoyo airily to the

young man, who could not believe his ears. "A little dieting will clean him out, which is what he needs."

Ti-Coyo found it difficult to grasp the fact that the hunchback should take it into his head to give the shark a purge, and he rubbed his ears to make sure that they were in their accustomed place and that he had heard correctly. Furthermore, the means Cocoyo had hit on to achieve this end— dieting—seemed to him to be wholly unsuited to sharks in general, and to a monster like Manidou in particular, who felt really in form only if he got at least a ton of nourishment each day.

"Did you say you wanted to give the shark a purge?" he asked incredulously, for he found it hard to believe that his father had ever taken Manidou to a vet for treatment.

"That's just what I said," replied Cocoyo severely. "Have you taken a look at his eyes?"

Ti-Coyo admitted, in some confusion, that he had not recently been paying much attention to Manidou's eyes, hearing which, the hunchback triumphantly retorted:

"Well, look at 'em! They're the eyes of somebody who's in need of a clean-out."

How the hunchback had reached this conclusion

was something that Ti-Coyo could not understand, and he set himself to examine, not the shark's eyes, as would perhaps have been natural, but his father's face, and what he saw there persuaded him to compromise.

"If you think," he began hesitatingly, "that Manidou really needs—"

"No one needs it more at this moment," the hunchback assured him seriously. "Just look at his eyes!"

Ti-Coyo said nothing. He thought it useless to ask his father whether he had taken the shark's pulse or looked at his tongue, or told him to cough and count up to ten. He decided that he would be better employed in going back to the house and heating up a second bowl of coffee, leaving Manidou impatiently thrashing about in the tank, with his nose glued to the grille, and wondering why they were so late in raising it this morning, this being the time when he ought to be setting off on urgent affairs of his own. Naturally, he could not guess that the hunchback had decided to give him a purge.

Ti-Coyo was extremely puzzled by the hunchback's advice, though not for the world would he show any curiosity. He knew his father too well not

to feel sure that if he was keeping the shark imprisoned in his tank, he must have some good reason
for doing so. Consequently, he abandoned all idea
of putting out to sea without his shark and remained
loafing about the plantation.

A little later Dora came home from market
greatly excited. "Where's the shark?" she cried out
between gasps (Ti-Coyo decided that she must have
been running). "The dead man's brother's rowing
about in the harbor with the magic gun in the bottom of his boat!"

Ti-Coyo gave a violent start, and gazed with an
expression of wonder and gratitude at the hunchback, who seemed not in the least surprised at the
news. He merely asked very calmly:

"Which of the fishermen's rowing him?"

"Not a fisherman around here would dare do
such a thing!" replied Dora vehemently. "The
man's brought a boat over from Basse Pointe. But
how comes it that the shark's still in his tank this
morning?"

Ti-Coyo began to explain with much seriousness
that the hunchback, after examining Manidou's
eyes and taking his pulse, had decided that what he
needed was to go on a diet for a day, and Dora in
her turn fixed an admiring eye on the cunning and

farseeing hunchback. The other eye, though no less
expressive of admiration, was focused in the opposite direction on a mango tree, which, conscious of
having done nothing to deserve such a stare, started
to wave its branches about in an embarrassed fashion.

Ti-Coyo, meanwhile, had drawn his knife from
its sheath and was testing its edge with great care on
the palm of his hand. The hunchback had no il-
lusions about the meaning of this innocent occupation at such a moment, and said quietly:

"Let him live a bit longer. After all, Manidou
can change his habits for a while and go hunting at
night. The man's a South African, and no doubt
he'll go back to his own country before long."

"Are you suggesting that I should let a stranger,
and the brother of a stranger, lay down the law
about what's to happen in St. Pierre harbor, and in
my shark's stomach?" asked the young man, baring
his white teeth like a great Dane flying at somebody's throat.

His voice was rancorous and angry. He found no
difficulty in understanding that the fishermen of St.
Pierre should have a grievance against the shark; he
readily admitted it. But the idea that two foreigners, who had turned up from heaven knew where,

should entertain such furious feelings for Manidou, who had in no way harmed their interests, whatever those might be, filled Ti-Coyo's heart with fury and hate.

The hunchback, however, managed, not without difficulty, to prevail on his son to consent to a delay in the execution of his homicidal design, much though it went against the young man's feelings.

"What point is there in waiting?" he asked, reluctantly returning the knife to its sheath. "This one's not going to follow you into the mountain."

"The spirits don't use knives," replied the hunchback calmly; "everybody knows that, even the police. Remember, it was the sea, not a man with a knife, that punished Nat the Mulatto, and the mountain the South African."

"And who, may I ask, is going to look after this chap?"

"That's for the spirits to decide," remarked the hunchback as he hobbled away self-importantly.

About an hour after midnight the hunchback crept silently out of his house and took the path leading to the Roxelane, the river that cuts St. Pierre into two parts. He was carrying a parcel under his arm. On the left bank stood the town's only hotel, in which the South African had his quarters, a room on the second floor with a wrought-iron balcony supported by caryatids.

The night was heavy and stifling, and Cocoyo was delighted to see, as he made his way through the deserted streets, that in almost every house he passed, the inhabitants had opened their windows.

He made good progress on his naked feet (he had left his shoes at home) and soon arrived under the South African's window. He reached the balcony by getting a grip on the charming white marble lady whose head held up the wrought-iron superstructure, showing the same agility as when he had clambered up the calabash tree in the forest clearing. The Roxelane ran close by, its waters gurgling round the great boulders that studded its course, occasionally imitating the stifled laughter of a woman tripping down a loosely cobbled street.

The window of the room, here as elsewhere, was open because of the great heat, and in the semidarkness the hunchback made out the figure of the South African, who, stretched at full length on his bed, with his mouth open, was snoring unpleasantly, giving the impression that he was tearing his throat to pieces.

Cocoyo proceeded to take from his hump, to

which it had been secured by a leather thong, the box that he had brought back with him from the mountain. He opened the lid and let the snakes, torpid from the action of the drug and from their long confinement, slip out onto the waxed parquet floor.

There they remained for a moment without stirring. Then they stretched themselves with little jerky movements of the head. Cocoyo had no wish to see more and slid down the caryatid to the ground. Then he hurried off on the way home.

He was not ignorant of the fact that, as soon as they smelled fresh water, the snakes would make off through the open window in the direction of the river, up which they would swim until they reached a patch of woodland or undergrowth in which they could feel at home. But he knew, too, that no matter how eager they might be to decamp, they would not leave without first taking the time to present their compliments to the man lying fast asleep in the bed.

Dora did not waste much time at the market next morning, but ran all the way home, arriving out of breath.

"The brother of the man with the magic gun is

dead too!" she announced, panting heavily. "He's been found stiff as a plank in his bed!"

"What did he die of?" asked the hunchback, breathing gently on the gold handle of his crop, and then rubbing it on the lapel of his jacket until it shone.

"Snakes—snakes—bit him!" stammered Dora, whose eyes were popping out of her head. "Nobody saw them; they struck and they vanished!"

"I didn't know," said Ti-Coyo slowly, looking the hunchback straight in the eyes, "that snakes put up at the hotel."

"It wasn't snakes," replied the hunchback seriously, "but the spirits of the river that punished this man, as the spirits of the mountain punished his brother, and the spirits of the sea Nat the Mulatto, because all of them dared to attack the shark!"

Dora said not a word, but from the fierceness of her squint it could be seen how deeply impressed she was by her husband's words.

Ti-Coyo walked down the path and raised the grille of the tank, where the shark was going round furiously in circles. Then he launched his canoe, calling back over his shoulder:

"Manidou says he's been cleaned out enough!"

"St. Pierre's been cleaned out, too," the hunch-back shouted back, making a face—"purged of our enemies!"

Dora slipped her arm through Cocoyo's, and the two of them stood there, their eyes pensively fixed on the canoe, which was moving out to sea with its sail bellying, and its hull heeling over until the gunwale was only a few inches above the water.

CHAPTER VIII

Surrounded by his wife, his son, and his grandson, comfortable in his magnificent house at the heart of his plantation, Cocoyo was completely happy. He wished for nothing—except a good sailing ship. The hunchback had not reached his advanced age only to find suddenly that he had a vocation for the sea. If he had set his heart on a sailing ship, the reason was to a high degree a commercial one.

Nobody could doubt that big ships no longer had

any use for the dilapidated harbor of a dead town. They passed proudly on their way, well out to sea off St. Pierre, making for Fort-de-France, where they now unloaded and loaded their cargoes.

Consequently, the hunchback, besides the cost of freightage, was obliged, in addition, to pay for cartage by road of the empty casks that he imported for his rum, and return them in the same manner, and with the same double expense, filled with the molasses that he sent to the neighboring islands.

Now, Cocoyo had a strong prejudice against squandering his money—it was the least of his faults —and this state of affairs was visibly getting on his nerves. He never tired of saying that "a planter should carry his goods in his own bottoms"; he said it so often that Ti-Coyo, sick of listening to his complaints on this score, begged Lucie to please his father by going through the columns of the various journals devoted to maritime affairs. Thus it was that she came, one day, on an advertisement of a ship for sale, of four hundred tons, which was lying in the harbor of Colón, where it was necessary to go to inspect it.

Ti-Coyo, much to the satisfaction of his father, expressed his willingness to see the business through, and two days later he took passage in Robert Fil de Fer's smack as far as Fort-de-France, where he purposed to take the first steamer leaving for Colón.

When they reached a point off shore from Case-Navire, whence they could see, at no great distance, the anchorage of Fort-de-France, Robert Fil de Fer, who was not by nature talkative and had not once opened his lips since they started, let go the oars for a moment, scratched his head thoughtfully, and observed that he wouldn't give a row of beans for either of their lives if his boat happened at that moment to turn turtle.

"Why?" asked Ti-Coyo casually. "The sea's calm, and we're close to land."

"There's a shark been following us ever since we left St. Pierre," answered the fisherman with a shudder, "and he must be the father of all the sharks born hereabouts for the last half century at least—I've never seen such a big one."

Ti-Coyo did not so much as bother to turn his head to glance at the great fin that was sticking out of the water no more than a hundred yards behind the smack, for he knew perfectly well the identity of that shark. Had he wished to make the trip unaccompanied, he would not have raised the grille of the tank just before starting. But he had thought it a good idea to take Manidou with him to Colón.

The monster did not often have such a chance of seeing the world and having fun. Besides, Ti-Coyo would feel less lonely during his eight-day trip if he knew that the shark was within easy call. He was very careful, therefore, to make quite sure an hour later, as he leaned over the rail of the liner lying at the wharf, that the shark, which had followed him thus far, would be able to see where he was going.

The liner's name was *Possenor*. She had just returned from Europe and was preparing to leave for Colón, where she would finish the trip, after calling at Fort-de-France. They weighed anchor early that afternoon.

Ti-Coyo visited every nook and cranny of the ship with the greatest curiosity. He could not get it into his head that he was on a ship at all; it seemed to him more like a first-class hotel, as far as possible from the sea.

Just as they drew away from the land, he leaned over the rail, not for the purpose of taking a last look at the capital, which was dropping astern in a gentle haze, but in order to make sure that the shark's fin was still visible. Manidou was splashing about to starboard with every sign of enjoyment, like a businessman setting out on a holiday, and the half-dozen passengers on deck pointed him out to one another with little shrieks of excitement.

The liner was not carrying many people, unless one counted the two or three dozen working folk from Martinique—men and women—who were bound for Colón to work in a shoe factory for which they had been engaged by contract.

Although Ti-Coyo had taken a first-class ticket, he did not bother about eating in the liner's big dining-saloon in company with gilt-edged ship's officers and passengers exhilarated by the extra-dry Mumm that was served as a matter of routine in honor of the Martinique landfall, the Sylvaner by which the fillets of eel were accompanied, and the heavy Saint-Émilion which brought out the flavor of the saddle of lamb which, in its turn, bolstered up the fish. This elaborate succession of wines was the result of the head steward's personal initiative. He was to wonder later whether he might not have been ill-advised to take such pride in this arrangement.

In any case, there was nothing on the menu to tempt Ti-Coyo's appetite—or even a more refined palate—and he ordered an underdone steak to be brought to him in his cabin. The weight of this chunk of red meat, when specified by Ti-Coyo, caused the maître d'hôtel to start when he took the order, and to hurry away at headlong speed. It was his first trip in this part of the world, and his facetious comrades had assured him before his departure that Martinique was inhabited by Caribbean cannibals. Hence it was a trembling scullion, escorted by two sailors armed with kitchen knives— and not the maître d'hôtel himself, who had taken the order—who finally brought to Ti-Coyo the four pounds of half-raw flesh.

After finishing his meal, the young man went on deck, where he stretched himself out in a deck-chair and was soon lost in dreams, after making sure that Manidou was still in the liner's wake.

Three days later, at about the same hour, Ti-Coyo was again in the same place—on deck and in the deck-chair, when he felt a light slap on his cheek. He was on his feet with one bound, looking at the sky and sniffing the breeze. He was familiar with that peculiar puff of air on his bare skin and realized what it meant. He hurried to the rail to see what had become of Manidou, but nowhere could he see a sign of the shark, who no doubt had picked up from the waves the same warning that the wind had brought to Ti-Coyo, and had made for the open sea in search of shelter.

The sound of voices and gusts of laughter reached Ti-Coyo from the saloon, and he told himself that it wouldn't be long before the passengers would be laughing on the other side of their faces. Then he went below to his cabin, where he lay down on his bunk to await what was coming.

That night the Caribbean Sea was celebrating the two-hundred-millionth anniversary of her birth (the captain had known nothing of this, otherwise he would have delayed the ship's departure), and had decided to give herself a little party to mark the occasion. She made a faint sign—both Ti-Coyo and the shark had noticed it—and the wind immediately began to show its virtuosity by embarking on a series of whistling modulations in different keys. This it carried through so successfully, with so many flourishes and variations on a theme known only to itself, that it seemed as though it must have acquired its skill from a human master; and as the wind has no lips, the miracle was all the more astonishing.

The whistling made a confused hubbub all around the steamer. The different tunes had now increased in number. They intermingled and swelled to a shrill din, urging one another on with a succession of piercing notes. A real concert was by this time under way, perfectly orchestrated, and so stirring that all the heavy-backed waves waiting in reserve just below the surface, and all the great swells slumbering on the bottom, hastened to the spot, jumping for joy, as soon as they heard the first bars summoning them to a wild ecstasy of dancing.

They could be heard coming in from far away with a noise of happy roaring. Troop after troop, they flung themselves upon the sea, which showed white at their approach, bringing with them huge masses of unemployed water which had been hanging about in the vicinity looking for a chance to have a bit of fun.

Pushed from behind, falling over one another, they hurried to where the *Possenor*—the very image of tranquillity—was forging ahead with all her engines thumping, doing her best to look unperturbed and behaving much like a child who sings aloud in the night to give itself courage.

Of all this the waves took no notice, but flung their full weight against the liner, which started to tremble, for all the world as though it were a frightened human—surrounding it with careless

gaiety, dealing it blow after blow from every side
with such effect that the hull shook from stem to
stern.

Then they tried to push their noses through the
portholes, and invaded the deck with the object of
adapting to their own use such deck-chairs as remained in position, dragging them back as they
withdrew, no doubt intending to keep them as sou-
venirs to show to their friends who were busy elsewhere.

Next they made a combined rush at the doors,
whose locks were in no condition to resist them, and
spread with a joyful gurgle over the floors of the
public rooms, where the furniture at once joined in
the dance, and, with feet in the water, banged so
roughly against the walls that it was quickly reduced to splinters.

Now and again the waves dashed violently
against the bridge, where, failing to dislodge the
captain, who had taken the precaution of lashing
himself to the rail, they whipped off his cap with
undue familiarity. Nor did they forget to deliver an
attack against the lifeboats, which, on both port and
starboard sides of the deck, were soon infected with
the same spirit of mad merrymaking and took steps
to smash the chains and cables by which they were

suspended and thus broke free from the davits in the hope of rejoining the waves. The latter lost no time in playfully and without malice turning them head over heels. Then they frolicked up against the derricks (which, being made of steel, failed to see the point of the joke) and streamed back again in cataracts to the scuppers, only to return a moment later to break over the deck with increased enjoyment.

The passengers in their cabins were by this time bent double over the basins, pulling the strangest faces. A few hours before, they had been laughing in the most carefree of moods, but laughter was the last thing they thought of now. They were busy concentrating their efforts, to an accompaniment of whines and whimpers, on getting rid of the more tasty morsels of their dinner. Between spasms they hastily dabbed their faces with extremely expensive Eau de Cologne. They coughed and struggled for breath. They were flung to right and to left by the pitching of the ship, and finally collapsed upon their bunks, but only temporarily, for they were soon struggling to their feet again and staggering with much retching and groaning to lean over the basins.

Finally, with nothing left in their stomachs, they

lay twisting and squirming, doubled up, sniveling, cursing the sea, and registering oaths that all their future traveling should be done by air.

But this threat had no effect upon the waves— since they were not stockholders in any of the shipping companies. On the contrary, they continued unceasingly to deliver attack after attack on the *Possenor,* which was shaking and creaking through all her length, dipping her nose and bringing it up again streaming with water, and abandoning all hope of keeping in the sea the great clumsy propeller, which, when the wind dropped for a few moments, could be heard revolving wildly in the air with a noise like the clanking of old iron. In fact, the *Possenor* was like a wet dog with a tin can tied to its tail.

The members of the crew, barefooted, ankle-deep in water, and avoiding as best they could the waves which were making free of the deck from end to end, staggered hither and thither with a great show of doing something, though in no way benefiting the ship.

Each time that the captain leaned forward on his bridge to shout an order into one of the speaking-tubes at his side, he was met with a smother of spray which so enveloped the mouthpieces of the instruments that he closed his mouth without having said anything, for no one likes having to swallow sea water. Not that anything the captain might, or might not, have shouted would have had the slightest effect, seeing that the waves had by now decided to do exactly as they liked.

The sea wished to make it clear to the men riding on her back that they were where they were, in their iron cockleshell filled with smoke, only because she consented to put up with them and was tolerating their presence in the middle of the sea— merely tolerating them, and not, as some of them seemed to think, admitting any right.

This was something of which everybody on board was, at the moment, convinced, and the passengers who, crouching in the corners of their cabins, and busy bringing up what they thought must be their very hearts and souls, would not have dreamed of questioning it. The sea, however, continued with her demonstration, hurling wave after wave, and then more, against the vessel, which shuddered under the impact of each assault.

Suddenly, no one knew from where, a gray and silent waterspout rudely assailed the *Possenor* on one side, while a second mass of water, till then held in reserve, struck her from the contrary direction, so that she found herself held tight between several million tons of water which showed themselves disinclined to loosen their hold upon the hull. There was no alternative open to the *Possenor* but to mount higher, and higher and higher—with the hearts of the passengers following deliberately in her terrifying climb.

But just as those mortal organs, it seemed to their owners, had reached their teeth (they kept their mouths tight shut so as to close the opening and prevent their hearts from getting clear away), the waterspouts made off, each taking its separate way, and the *Possenor* had no choice but to start going down again into the bottomless abyss that now opened beneath her keel. But this change of direction brought no gain to the passengers. From time to time an unruly surge, bearing down on the ship from full ahead, struck her so violently upon the bows that she came to a sudden standstill, as though a mortal blow had been dealt her, after which she began to move once more through the sea. Her progress was like that of a corpse drained of all life, and without so much as a tremor, because the engines down below, stunned by the shock, had ceased to turn.

Then the men in the stokehold made haste to

raise the pressure, and slowly, regretfully, the throbbing became once more apparent, though it brought no comfort to the ship or to anyone on board.

And now it happened that the wind broke off in the very middle of one of its worst shrieking-bouts, which ended in an odd sort of gurgle, as though the blast had been seized by the throat and was struggling for breath. The sea, too, stopped its roaring, seemingly unsure of what had happened. The liner, at this, recovered some small amount of confidence. She lay clumsily riding the sea and creaking with relief, so that in the stillness that followed, all sorts of furtive noises became audible, the exact nature of which it would have been hard to define, though they were so familiar to the listening ear that in the silence they sounded a reassuring note.

The interval of calm lasted sometimes five minutes or more, and everyone—except Ti-Coyo, still stretched out in his cabin, who knew the extent of the sea's cunning—began to think that the gale had blown itself out. But then the wind, no doubt rested, gave vent to a whole series of furious shrieks, and the waters returned to the attack with a short roar. The *Possenor,* well aware of what that meant, uttered a long-drawn moan, as though hoping to win sympathy from the sea. But the sea—as the liner should have known—feels sympathy for no one but itself, and returned to the charge so violently, and with so deafening a din, that it gave the impression of being eager to make up for lost time, and of wanting to wipe out the very memory of its momentary lull. Whereupon the battered ship, flung upwards, and assailed on all sides by the waves, rose in the air, lurching despairingly, and then, as the result of a particularly vicious attack, plunged downward into watery darkness.

As for the barometer, it seemed determined at all costs to have nothing to do with what was going on. It had been still at "Set Fair" some minutes before the hurricane burst, and was no doubt thoroughly put out at having been caught off its guard. All it did now was to drop a few degrees, after which, deciding that this slight concession was all that could be expected of it, it moved no farther.

Its "flair" had been proved wrong, and that, of all things, is what most infuriates barometers—a normal reaction, to be sure, on their part, for they have nothing in the world to do but keep an accurate watch on the weather. Besides, this particular barometer had a strong dislike of Caribbean hurricanes—which always arrive unannounced, never give warning of their coming—and made nothing of its vigilance.

Naturally enough, the ship's officers were only too ready to seize this opportunity to call it opprobrious names and to allude to the services it might have rendered in words deeply wounding to the self-respect of a barometer belonging to a three-funneled liner of one of the great ocean-going fleets. And so it was that it swung sulkily on its nail each time anyone looked like consulting it. The captain had already, on three separate occasions, turned his back on it with a shrug, which is the worst insult that can be given to a ship's barometer.

The members of the crew had by now taken shelter in the most protected of their duty stations and were playing cards. There was nothing else for them to do at the moment. Playing cards was nothing. The real problem was how to shuffle the cards and deal them, both operations needing two hands if they were to be performed successfully. Anyone who even for a moment let go of whatever he was clinging to was inevitably flung to the deck (the lurching of the vessel saw to that), to the delight of his companions. Consequently, though everybody wanted to play, nobody wanted to deal—and the sailors had great fun.

A very different state of mind obtained in the galleys, where one half of the kitchen staff were being racked by spasms of seasickness, while the other half were busy feverishly buckling the straps of their safety belts around their shoulders and waists. For cooks and their assistants have this in common with rats, that they are always anxious to be the first off a ship when danger threatens.

CHAPTER IX

FROM KEEL to mizzenmast, from wheelhouse to winch, every port and parcel of the liner was shrieking aloud in anguish, while the driven spray streamed ceaselessly down masts and funnels, like sweat down the face of a man in agony. Sometimes a great ground-swell emerged from the vasty depths and dizzily expanded beneath the hull, which it raised higher and higher toward the sky, giving the impression that it was trying to placate with this offering some angry god concealed behind the low clouds. When this happened, the *Possenor,* her propeller threshing the air with a clattering din, creaked all over and groaned in her misery.

Occasionally two waves would crash down upon her simultaneously from port and starboard, meeting with a savage shock in the very middle of her deck, where, oblivious of all else, they engaged in a life-and-death struggle for what appeared to be a point of precedence—surging hither and thither, swaying together breast to breast, each concerned only to make the other withdraw and to force its own way forward, while, above the fight, their white and heavy crests, like hair, streamed in the tempest. This went on until a new lot of waves, assuming from the noise made by the ship's propeller desperately revolving in the air that the way forward was clear, dashed in their turn across the deck, where they reconciled the two antagonists and kept a space around them clear.

But they did not withdraw without taking something with them—a door that had been wrenched from its hinges, a table or a chair caught up in their passage through the saloons, and now seen spinning giddily in the spume, dancing wildly in the wake of the surge, breaking through the rail without being smashed in the process, or leaving only some part of themselves behind. The linen, too, played a part in the wild caracole—napkins torn from tea-trays and opening upon the surface of the sea like multi-colored flowers, cushions swept against their will from sofas, hangings and carpets which the waves had been at great trouble to collect from restau-rants, bars or reading-rooms, though it was far from clear what use they intended to make of these odds and ends once they had got them.

But the liner was not yet at the end of her troubles, for the sea had received reinforcement in the shape of a thunderstorm which, jerked awake by the din below, thought it only polite to join in the merriment, which it proceeded to do without wasting a moment.

Lightning shot from the heavens like blades of blue steel and drove obliquely into the body of the darkness, which responded to the repeated stabs with a prolonged shuddering. The author of these gleaming knife-thrusts at once expressed his satis-faction with deafening oaths, which stuck for a mo-ment in his throat before leaping helter-skelter through his gaping mouth. Again and again he brandished his bare and glittering blades, again and again roared his happy oaths. And so it went on, for he showed no sign of fatigue, nor spared a scrap of mercy for the wounded night, which made no effort to avoid the blows, and felt its black blood flow without uttering a single cry.

Whereupon the wind redoubled its whistling, playing variations on its own violence, and the waves, obedient to the summons, drove forward with ten times their former eagerness.

Meanwhile, the first mate, having set off on a tour of inspection round the ship, returned to the bridge and informed the captain that the steerage passengers from Martinique, who were on their way to work in Colón, had organized a ball in honor of one of their number whose birthday it happened to be, and were dancing away in their dining-hall, precisely as they would have done in the shade of their native mango trees, without paying the slightest attention to the hurricane. Two of them were beating rhythmically with the palms of their hands on an open soap-box in time to the noise (the mate couldn't call it a tune) which a third was producing from a clarinet.

It had needed only this to set all the others, men and women, swaying their hips and jigging up and down in the most unseemly manner. The pitching of the vessel, the mate added, with a look of disgust, kept flinging them against one another, and now and then sent them sprawling on the deck. But whenever this happened, they scrambled up again at once, grinning, and returned at once to their contortions.

As to the other passengers, they were all shut in their cabins, nor could there be any doubt what they were doing there. This time the mate went through the movement of leaning forward and clutching his stomach.

The mate was a fine-looking man with a dignified air who was regarded by his friends as the life and soul of any party, and he did everything he could, when dealing with his social equals, to deserve this enviable reputation.

The captain shook his head, and the mate went off to continue his tour of inspection. The door of the cabin, caught by a gust, violently slammed shut behind him, and no sooner had he started to lurch down the narrow staircase leading from the bridge to the deck than a roller coming in late to the attack swept over him without a word of warning and, as it looked as though he was going to cling to the handrail, proceeded to carry away the whole of the staircase, which previous pommeling had left in a shaky condition.

Somebody hailed the captain through the loud-speaker in a corner of the cabin, and by putting his ear to the instrument he could just manage to recognize the voice of the purser. One word out of three reached him of what the purser was saying. By the time he had finished what he had to say, the captain was in possession of official information to the effect that fire had broken out aboard. The purser held the lightning responsible for this new catastrophe.

The captain had every intention of going down on deck to see with his own eyes what truth there was in the news, but when he attempted to do so, he realized that he was a prisoner on his own bridge, the companionway having completely vanished. But it never occurred to him that the first mate—much against his will—had set off to take a walk on the sea in company with the said companionway, and in such inclement weather, or that he had been dragged off by a surge of water which was in a thoroughly bad temper as a result of having found nothing more important to carry away than a rickety set of stairs to which a clean-shaven man in oilskins was clinging.

.   .   .

The liner was toiling and moiling, rolling and fighting for breath, and it looked as though each new onset of the waves would finish her altogether. She managed, however, to pull herself together, though scarcely had her bows emerged from the flurry of rollers when she was forced down again and disappeared behind a wall of water, this time, it seemed, for good.

The wind had picked up from heaven knew where an unpublished score, which it opened in the darkness and proceeded to play with a dash and a fire which even the captain, had he not been preoccupied with his own situation on the bridge, and that of his ship on the water, could not but have applauded.

As it was, the storm, filled with admiration, and no doubt with a wish to compete, suddenly set the sky ablaze with green light—for all the world like the most wonderful firework effect—which precipitated from the obscurity an avalanche of black clouds. With such rapidity did the thunderclaps follow one another that even Ti-Coyo, stretched out on his berth in his cabin, and with experience of more than one hurricane and more than one thunderstorm, could not help feeling surprised.

The display started far away with a noise that resembled the sound of great stones rolling down a tin roof, came nearer, and was amplified until it burst suddenly in a deafening roar. Then it was that the sea, not to be outdone, gave a fresh impetus to its own voice and its billows, so as to be in harmony with the general orchestral performance, and to please somebody, though not the liner.

Every now and again, as though the tempest and the thunder were not making enough noise as it was, could be heard, through the whistling of the wind and the explosive activities of the lightning, a long-drawn-out and decidedly vulgar note from the clarinet with which the musician from Martinique was keeping his compatriots in the steerage dancing.

It was no use saying anything to them. They were a touchy lot who were ready at the slightest excuse to make reference to their knives in far from polite terms. Besides, they had been free to stage their ball at the very moment when the other passengers had found it necessary to succumb to sickness and to tremble on their legs. The purser had been careful not to interfere. It had occurred to him that it might be a good thing to have a drink, and with this end in view he made his way to the bar. There he found the bartender half-crazed behind the counter and, having mixed a cocktail for himself, proceeded to concoct some sort of brew which he tried to make the bartender swallow, seeing that the man was quite genuinely in bad shape.

But the latter seemed for the moment to prefer dying to opening his lips, for he had good reason to guess what might happen if he was foolish enough to do any such thing. As for drinking anything whatever, the very idea made him retch, and he met the purser's kindly insistence with a mute appeal for mercy.

All the bartender wanted was to be left alone. He could not remember ever having hurt anybody since the day he was born, except his mother, perhaps, when he was cutting his first teeth. He begged the purser, in the name of everything he held most dear, to clear off as quickly as possible with his mixture, the very sight and smell of which—particularly the smell—filled him with nausea. In order, however, that he might make his meaning clear, it was necessary for him to open his lips at least the fraction of an inch, even to whisper. The worst happened, and the purser had only just time to jump back before the bartender, now at his last gasp, abandoned the struggle that he had been carrying on with his stomach since the gale began, in the hope of retaining, at all costs, what he had absorbed during the course of the evening.

The smell of tobacco, too, made him sick. It is surprising how demanding people become when they are feeling out of sorts, and the bartender, as soon as the purser began to light a cigarette, indicated by signs that he would very much prefer him to do his smoking somewhere else. That was easily said, but the number of places where a man might take a stroll was limited. In fact, the cabins, the first-class bar, and perhaps the second-class lounge and restaurant were about the only places that had not been flooded. Consequently, the purser decided, at the risk of incurring the wordless curses that showed in the bartender's eyes, to stay where he was and smoke in relative peace and quiet.

The wind now let out two or three long, piercing whistles, as though to rally and encourage its followers, and, from the way in which the ship was immediately set trembling, it was easy to see that each one had responded to the appeal.

The waves were busy combining their forces preparatory to delivering a frontal attack, as though everything they had done so far had been no more than a pleasant loosening-up exercise designed to get them into proper condition for the serious work ahead.

This time they began to batter away in good earnest at the liner. They no longer attempted to swallow it up as they had previously done, but contented themselves with bludgeoning the hull—bow, stern, port, and starboard—everywhere, in fact, where there was anything left to bludgeon—going to it with the regularity of a sledgehammer and the patience of a blacksmith.

The *Possenor* was now taking part in the dance with a will. No longer did she confine herself to groaning and rolling, but started to jump about as if she were no more than an abandoned canoe, to hop, indeed, like a cat on hot bricks, so that the thin red line painted on her keel became visible. Then she started to dive, with a clumsy rollicking movement, until there was nothing to be seen upon the surface but the extreme tips of her three funnels, which continued, quite peacefully, to emit their smoke. When she emerged from the furrow, with the water cascading noisily from her bridge, the waves returned to their task of battering at the hull. It seemed incredible that they should not already have knocked it to pieces.

The liner had lost way entirely since the tempest

had begun, and was now merely wallowing at the mercy of the sea. She had gone a long way off her course, the captain told the purser, who with great difficulty and by dint of hauling himself up by some dangling ropes during a brief lull had succeeded in reaching the bridge.

But that was not the full extent of the danger, because the latter maintained that he had located the fire somewhere near the barbershop. It had been impossible to make sure of this, because, owing to the waves, nobody could reach that part of the ship, which had been almost continuously submerged for the last few hours, that, perhaps, being the reason why the fire had made no progress. It might even by this time have been extinguished— extinguished by the waves, which for once would have done something worth doing and made themselves useful. But the purser was convinced that he had seen a lot of smoke in the hairdressing-saloon— where it had no business to be—drifting in black coils through the cracks of the door.

The captain declared that he must go and see what really was happening, and the purser shrugged his shoulders. He knew well enough that there was nothing to be seen, nothing for the time being to be done, and that they would be far better employed in staying where they were, and might consider themselves fortunate in being able to do so. The captain gripped the doorknob, and it did not take him long to realize that it was jammed. A heavy sea must have been responsible for that. In spite of all his efforts, seconded by those of the purser, the door refused to budge. The only way of getting it open was by taking an ax to it, or blowing the lock off with a revolver, but neither of these weapons happened to be available. Furthermore, the bridge was now under water for most of the time, and, as the result of some accident, the speaking-tubes had been blocked up, or broken, in some other way. The captain, therefore, isolated on his bridge and held prisoner in his own cabin, was, in some sort, cut off from his ship. He could no more hope to communicate with his crew than if he had been marooned in some port five hundred miles away.

This he finally had to admit, and returned with a gloomy look on his face to the metal rail to which both he and the purser were forced to cling if they wished to remain on their feet. At this moment the purser, chancing to look up, realized from the captain's expression—he was busy peering through the porthole, though there was little enough to be seen in the darkness—that something unusual was happening. He was just opening his mouth to question his superior officer when he was flung violently onto the berth opposite, from which he rolled to the floor on top of the captain, who was already stretched out full-length there. He could not remember having let go of the metal handrail, and saw with surprise that it had been torn loose by the shock and was still in his hands.

Something—the captain later described it as a gigantic column of black water standing upright on the sea without any means of support, though this the purser did not believe—something dark and flabby with a sort of curling tip at its highest point where it touched the low-hanging clouds, was moving toward the ship. A flash of lightning had enabled the captain to get a clear view of this object (he had never seen anything like it before) almost at the moment when it made contact with the ship, forcing the bows into the air and holding her immobilized, stuck up on end.

All noise suddenly ceased. Wind, waves, and even the thunder seemed to be holding their breath, while the *Possenor* tried desperately to achieve a solid stance on the sea, her superstructure quivering without a moment's respite, and creaking with the effort she was making. Then, from high in the heavens, a mass of water crashed heavily down upon the vessel, which shuddered to its very keel-plates before collapsing under the weight, like a huge, rigid, inert body in which there was no longer any sign of life.

It was hot in the cabin, where there was no longer any light. But the darkness outside was now less dense, and looked as though it were shot through by a sort of half light that came, not from the sky, where the heavy black clouds still hung in compact masses, but from the sea itself, which appeared to be lit up from inside by some mysterious fire.

The first thing of which the purser, lying crumpled up under the bunk, was aware was the cracking of the captain's joints when he scrambled to his feet, trying to find something to hold to. The purser was overcome by shame at the sight of his superior officer's highly polished boots within a few inches of his face, and he tried to crawl out from under the bunk. The captain was not paying the least attention to him. He was standing absolutely motionless, his features fixed in an expression of anxious waiting for no one knew what. Perhaps he was just stupefied, and the purser, who by this time had recovered his wits, thought it scarcely to be wondered at if he was.

Next a faint trembling ran through the *Possenor,* followed by one considerably more violent. The ship had been attacked by a prolonged fit of the staggers, like a man coming out of a faint. At the same moment one of the lights in the cabin ceiling came on again. The purser, seeing the captain's face relax, realized that he had been wondering all this time whether the life had gone out of his ship for good and all.

The liner had taken the initiative in breaking the surrounding immobility and silence, with the result that the thunderstorm, no doubt encouraged and emboldened by her example, began once more to mutter away behind the clouds, addressing fierce curses at somebody (it could scarcely be the captain, who had played no part in the recent occurrences), meanwhile flooding the spaces of the sky with innumerable flashes. The wind, too, to make up for its brief failure to live up to its reputation, resumed its whistling, though it seemed to have lost something of its earlier self-confidence, so that the sea, at first, turned a deaf ear to its appeals for help.

During all the time that this hesitation on the

part of the elements continued, the two men on the bridge, and even Ti-Coyo in his cabin, were conscious of feeling more hopelessly flattened out than at any time since the waves had started their lunatic dance. In fact, every living creature on board the liner felt, all of a sudden, inexpressibly and inexplicably tired out. Even the sailors had ceased to take any pleasure in their card game. The temperature was not excessive, and certainly had nothing to do with this sudden lethargy. It seemed, rather, as though the column of water—if, indeed, there had been a column of water—had left behind it an atmosphere of lassitude to which all had succumbed, not excluding the elements.

So marked was this that when, after interminable minutes during which the wind gradually recovered its breath, and the thunder resumed its banging about in the clouds, the sea again gave voice with a full-throated roar, flinging itself against the liner, which began again its heavy pitching, Ti-Coyo, together with everybody else on board, experienced an absurd feeling of relief at being once more up to the neck in the tempest— the warm, living tempest, which bayed and slobbered and rushed hither and thither in a fury of movement, for all the world like a wild beast with a hundred thousand mouths through which to howl, and as many feet on which to run about the sea. But as to the flabby and fantastic object that lifted ships out of the water, held them up on end above the sea, and then made off without a word—the captain had never imagined that such a thing could exist, and was trembling all over at the recollection of it.

The *Possenor* resigned herself to being pommeled by the waves and lashed by heavy seas and squalls of rain. It was once more possible to hear occasional whines from the clarinet of the man from Martinique, and the captain muttered a curse under his breath for the benefit of those who could go so far in idiosyncrasy—and insolence—as to continue to dance after all that had happened, whereas he himself wanted nothing but to fling himself fully dressed upon his bunk and stay there until the ship reached port.

The purser, who could not long resist talking to his companion, now asked him what he thought it was that the ship had run into, to which the captain replied that he had no idea—all he hoped was that nobody, and no ship either, would ever come across its like.

The storm had chosen that moment to make off, to moan and grouse under other skies. The lightning flashes had become fewer, the thunderclaps less frequent, and this led, after an hour had passed, to the wind making up its mind to seek another theater of operations. While it was thinking things over, hesitating to depart, and vaguely regretting the fact that the liner was still afloat, the heavy black clouds split apart, all at the same moment, as though at a word of command, and the wind, not much minding whether or not it got wet, decided to take an unhurried leave of the scene, whistling a pretty little tune, which it improvised as it went along.

The deep ground-swell and the waves, now ceasing to torment the ship, tumbled in a fine disorder in her wake, dancing gaily on her heels, for it had occurred to them—and not without reason— that the fun was bound to start all over again in some other part of the sea, where, no doubt, they would find other ships worthy of their attention.

As soon as the hurricane had been swallowed up far enough ahead to make it quite certain that it would not try to retrace its steps, silence fell quietly on the sea, covering it with a mantle of peace. The liner had by now recovered its stability and was again moving forward at its normal speed. All around, the rollers had subsided, more or less, into little waves, like dogs whipped to heel, and at the same time the last eddies of spume sheered off.

Freed from the black clouds with which its face had been daubed, the moon, all freshly powdered, and shining as brightly as a new guinea, resumed its mincing way across the sky, lighting up the drenched and devastated deck, which was now cluttered with every sort of oddment left there by the recent turmoil. Part of the water that had been shipped still rippled about the deck and streamed through the scuppers from stem to stern.

Ti-Coyo, who felt stifled in his cabin, now hastened up on deck for a breath of air, and because he wanted to see what the ocean looked like, and whether it seemed at all ashamed (naturally, no such thought occurred to it) at the damage caused by its recent behavior. He wondered what had happened to the shark, and whether it had found safe shelter in this stretch of sea, with which, doubtless, it was making its first acquaintance. Ti-Coyo gazed with wonder at the torn and twisted rigging, at the loose ends of ropes and cables hanging from the places where once the boats and life-belts had been. The deck was covered with planks and scraps of broken glass, and the young man could not help asking himself how the sea had managed to tear loose, and sometimes to carry away altogether, the brass plates which had seemed to be so firmly fastened to the rails.

The captain and the purser had resumed their struggle—a life-and-death struggle—with the handle of the cabin door. But the handle had come off best, and both men's shirts were soaked with sweat.

The captain had found in a drawer, and at once transferred to his bald head, a high cap belonging to his full-dress uniform (the storm had carried away the one he had been wearing previously), with just the right number of bands to which his rank entitled him, and considerably more in the matter of gold lace. This done, and as though he had found fresh strength in his new headdress, or as though the gold braid with which it was adorned had strengthened his faith in his rights and privileges, and in the propriety of his immediate intentions—which consisted in getting out of the cabin at any price—he started again to do battle with the doorknob.

None could have foreseen the issue of this mighty struggle, nor whether, in the long run, victory would go to the captain or the handle, if a passing sailor had not heard the captain's curses, broken down the door with a hatchet, and so released him.

Suddenly Ti-Coyo stood stock-still and pricked up his ears. At the same moment the vibrations made by the engines assumed a broken and a slower rhythm, until the liner ceased to move forward. At the same time the lights went out all over the ship, which was plunged in darkness.

In the stern of the vessel a tiny pink flame flared and flickered. She died down, only to reappear in the same spot. This time she was just a little, a very little, less narrow, but she flickered just as she had done before, though there was not much wind —flickered continuously and shook with fever, turning anxiously from side to side as though she had arrived late at some rendezvous, and was hoping against hope that the friend she was expecting would turn up after all. For she really was waiting for somebody, who was not slow in appearing.

Just as she was feverishly leaning down toward the deck and shivering, another nimble little flame, her very image in all respects, leaped into life only a few inches away, seemingly as anxious as she was about something, though it was impossible to say what.

"That was a celebration—a real celebration."

The two little flames positively flung themselves
into each other's arms and, for a good five minutes, gave every sign of extravagant happiness
—indulged in manifestations of the wildest delight
—hugging and stroking each other, drawing back for
a good look as a mother might do after having been
long parted from her child, just to make sure that
he has not changed—taking one another in from
head to foot with admiring glances, and then, in a
renewed access of endearments, kissing and embracing, clasping hands with charming, old-world for-
mality, bowing and curtsying.

"Darling! . . . how lovely you're looking! . . .
Quite perfect!"

"Nenni! What nonsense. But how that hairdo
does suit you! . . . Really, you look so sweet I
could gobble you up!"

Then they drew apart once more, controlling
their feelings in the most genteel fashion, only
again to come together, and again to separate,
jumping up and down on their tapering toes, which
had gone blue with the violence of their emotion.
They had all the exquisite and formal grace of ancient figures in a stained-glass window, but at the

same time an extraordinary freshness, a fantastic and febrile activity.

All the same, their agitation (which was extreme), and the way in which they turned and twisted in all directions, made it quite clear that they were expecting company—though, for the moment, their effusive greetings had put everything else out of their minds—other members of the family, no doubt, for no one has more relations than fire.

A moment later Ti-Coyo was in a position to note that this family party consisted of three large red flames—three important personages—who jumped across the planking of the deck, dragging at their heels a group of young pink-complexioned cousins who almost immediately vanished from view.

The arrival of these newcomers had the effect of brilliantly lighting up one corner of the deck, which enabled the young man to see that the captain, the purser, and most of the other officers were now on the scene. Round them was a confused crowd of sailors, all making gestures which had the air of being vastly mysterious because they were being made in the dark.

Meanwhile, the three large red flames did not stand by, doing nothing. They set to with a will clearing a path down which, in a short while, a lot of other relations crowded forward. A fire's family is past counting, and each of the fresh arrivals, even the least important, seemed to have the power of dividing at will into cousins once, twice, and three times removed, who, in their turn, apparently possessed the faculty of subdividing still further into a practically infinite number of other cousins, down to those of the twentieth and even the hundredth degree.

The party had moved scarcely at all from the place of their first meeting, and from beneath the deck now came the sound of a tune that was clearly a great favorite with them.

It was no more than a sort of mumble over a wheezy, muted ground-bass. This was followed by a crackling, the kind of sound made by a singer suffering from a frog in his throat. For a moment or two nothing was audible but this combination of crackling and dry coughing.

When it died down a bit, the hummed refrain was taken up again, accompanied by the rhythmic beat of the great pumps that were laboring away in the deep darkness underneath.

CHAPTER X

QUITE SUDDENLY, and as though someone had issued
the order: "All hands on deck," the rest of the imprisoned family turned up—the uncle with money
to leave, all green side-whiskers and scarlet paunch,
who swept across the deck and began to lick the
foremost of the three funnels, and the young folk
with pale, drooping shoulders, who strove in vain
to follow his brilliant example.

From all sides came a swarm of nephews and

145

grandnephews of every size and color, who fell furiously on every edible object—stays, rigging, odds and ends of broken furniture, anything, in fact, that happened to be lying about, down to the very life-belts hanging on the partitions—such of them, that is, as had escaped the violence of the waves.

Some of the ladies were so old that they were bent double and could do little more than creep along at deck-level. But they had their allotted task, which was to gnaw and sap and contrive an opening for the others to jump through with every sign of eagerness. There were, too, a number of dowagers present—very stiff, very dignified, and giving the impression that they were gazing at the scene through nonexistent lorgnettes, until a gust of wind tickled them up a bit, whereupon they at once lost their haughty bearing and seemed to go quite mad, twisting and twirling in the most ridiculous manner.

The teen-agers of the company, beribboned like so many pink and violet archbishops, set themselves with grim determination to clamber up to the captain's bridge, but were brought up short before they could reach it, because the larger flames snapped at them so savagely, and elbowed them

out of the way so roughly, that they were soon lost
to view, while a number of young girls with flushed
faces and blatantly dyed hair engaged in a rough-
and-tumble with several flat-chested youths: pale
tongues of fire which flickered and swooned like
enraptured lovers.

Sly babies there were as well—no higher than
that!—who clung to the skirts of their mothers (full-
figured matrons with glowing cheeks), or slipped
in and out between their parents' legs, hopeful of
getting hold of something secretly—a half-burned
plank, still smoking, which the long flames had neglected to burn completely, in their hurry to get
at a fresh supply of food—and young brides blush-
ing under their veils of fluttering tulle, clinging
to the arms of loutish youths eighteen and a half
feet tall, blazing with pride in their red jackets—
and maids of honor in scarlet dresses with striped,
self-satisfied escorts—and saturnine elders tottering
about the deck, looking as though they had forgotten their crutches—and devout women in white
tuckers, who furtively sketched a genuflection when
the wind was busy elsewhere.

There were austere great-aunts with yellow faces,
extending and retracting their skinny necks like
tortoises—and women of fashion with disheveled

hair who, for some reason known only to themselves, were engaged in scattering, like tragedy
queens, their loveliest jewels, their most superb
adornments—refulgent sparks and glowing brands
which vanished in the seas, and fell hissing in the
path of the liner.

The whole collection roared and raged, leaping
about the deck with a crackling and sputtering
which sounded like derisive laughter, its members
intertwined and utterly confused, trampling one another underfoot, and then again wriggling free.

Occasionally a flame that had disobeyed orders
would break away from the main body in order
to start clambering toward some patch of wood-
work which, in spite of the wind, it had been pa-
tiently courting, until, at the last moment, after
many unsuccessful advances, it managed to clasp it
in a triumphant embrace. At moments some late-
comer, richly decked out and crowned with a multicolored wig, would manage to force his way with
uncertain steps into the roaring chaos, where he
soon vanished. At others, willowy young creatures,
with the fairest of fair hair, would curl themselves
with a die-away look round the ship's steel masts
which they roused to a white heat.

At intervals the whole family party would withdraw a few steps to see how the work was progressing, with an impatient shaking of heads and scattering of sparks.

On the outskirts, a small group of brightly colored sprites was engaged in a laughing game of ring-o'-roses. These were the genii of the fire. Their foreheads were surmounted by stiff plumes of jade, or adorned with great single cabochon rubies, too heavy for their frail little bodies to support. Others waved aloft jagged and streaming crests, each scallop of which terminated in a different precious stone, here a sapphire, there a turquoise or a quivering emerald, which gave to these tiny folk a fairylike appearance. They took no part in the general mêlée, but kept themselves at a distance, drawing back when the others pressed too closely upon them, or even showed an inclination to come their way. They seemed to be excessively eager to remain in isolation, anxious only to get on with their game and their separate flickering. In this they showed how different they were from certain near-by flames who could not, it appeared, spare a thought for anything but eating and destroying.

They were so tiny that it was not difficult for them to avoid the gusts of wind, and they could proudly nose their way into places where the large tongues of flame, driven about wildly by the gale, lost their balance and their arrogance.

The increasing heat brought the rats out from their hiding-places, and they could be seen slipping about in the scuppers and running from the licking fire, which was now all round them. The liner was lit up as though for a gala, and the surrounding sea showed every color from the most subtle shades of pink to the most glaring crimson.

Suddenly that portion of the deck where the first two pink little flames had met collapsed with a roar, carrying with it all who happened to be standing near. Ti-Coyo saw the captain disappear over the edge of the boiling crater, still wearing on his bald head the high-crowned cap all aglitter with gold. Other shadowy figures, too, had vanished down the gaping hole in the deck, from which now the fire was leaping together with a huge cloud of evil-smelling smoke, which the wind, awakened by this heaven-sent gift, began to chase with chilly gusts toward the east.

The conflagration, no doubt, had broken out in the smoking-room, whence it had spread to the barbershop, the linen-room, and the holds. There it had gained fresh vigor, which had enabled it, in spite of the cold-storage installation (which it had taken in its stride), to reach the engine-room, where it had found in abundance everything necessary on which to proliferate and feed its voracious and insatiable family—the same family that had been allowed out on deck as soon as the two little pink and youthful flames (trained in the craft of scouting) had made sure that it and everything on it were good to eat.

There was nothing more to be done, and the thudding of the pumps all of a sudden stopped.

CHAPTER XI

Ti-coyo would never grow tired of watching so
extraordinary a spectacle, even when he heard a
series of significant "plouffs!" away to port—
the sound of a heavily laden boat dropping into the
water.

The passengers from Martinique had decided
that the time had come to stop their dancing and
think about saving their lives. They had at once
taken possession of two out of the remaining six

lifeboats without encountering any opposition. The clarinet-player, as self-appointed leader, had bustled about the deck, giving advice, helping to stow baggage, pointing out to each the best place, pushing along late-comers in a friendly way with his instrument, which he kept in his hand. One after another—women first—the company, without showing the slightest surprise, settled quietly into the boats. When the clarinet-player, in his turn, clambered aboard, and the men bent to the oars, he put his instrument to his lips and drew from it a tune as old as his native island, which the others all took up in chorus—being prevented by lack of space from continuing their dance—and their voices, astonishingly true and warm-toned, gradually were lost in the darkness along with the boats that were busy getting clear of the burning liner.

Ti-Coyo now settled down to think things out seriously.

St. Pierre was a long way off, and it would doubtless take him days and days to get there if he was reduced to swimming—with nothing to eat or drink and no chance of sleeping. Such a trip made in the existing circumstances would, he feared, be sadly lacking in amenities.

There was always a chance, too, that he might

fall in with ugly customers on the journey. Manidou, surely, would keep close to him the whole distance, but it was possible that he might be attacked by several sharks at once, and he had no wish to lose a limb in the adventure. He had urgent need of all those he possessed, and felt very much disinclined to say good-by to any of them. One pair of each was certainly not too much for the constant and various uses to which he put them.

He might equally well be attacked by a couple of giant turtles. Even a single one of these creatures weighed more than six hundred pounds, and no knife, however sharp, would be of any avail against their armored casing. In such an event Manidou could do little more than make a diversion by shouldering them aside.

Ti-Coyo had heard tell, too, of certain stingrays with pointed heads who haunted these waters, and had an unpleasant habit of turning into darting spears their yard-long tails, which ended in a couple of inches of unpleasant barb stuffed full of deadly poison. Both these creatures, the giant turtle and the stingray, were as vicious-minded as a cabaret singer out of a job.

Alternatively, just opposite to where he was, a lifeboat was still hanging, which, try as they might, the waves had not yet succeeded in wrenching loose from its davits, and it would provide him with a means of reaching St. Pierre without fatigue and keeping his feet and his backside dry. Care was usually taken to provision these boats and it was unlikely that he would perish of either hunger or thirst on the way. He might even be able to snatch forty winks at the tiller if the wind was favorable. Manidou could swim behind.

The hurricane had left intact only one boat in ten, and if he waited any longer before staking out a claim to this one, a crowd of persons—sailors or passengers—would certainly turn up before long determined to get hold of it at any price.

Consequently, Ti-Coyo climbed as nimbly as a cat into the boat suspended above his head. No sooner had he begun to manipulate the pulleys than it glided slowly down the liner's side in the direction of the sea.

Just as it hit the surface with a splash, there was a sound of running feet on the deck above, and, by raising his head, he could see a dozen or so cooks and kitchen boys leaning over the rail, shaking their fists and swearing at him.

"Ho!" he thought. "A good thing that I got hold of this tub when I did!"

At this moment one of the kitchen boys, half mad with rage and panic, climbed over the rail and jumped into the sea, in the hope of catching up with the boat. Ti-Coyo stopped rowing and sat with his oars in the air. The kitchen boy was very young, and people of his age, or even older, have no great wish to die.

But there was the shark to consider. Ti-Coyo began to wonder just how far he had a right to deprive Manidou, who could not be far away, of so attractive a meal. After all, Manidou had shown great consideration in staying with him, and Ti-Coyo did, he felt, owe him some practical form of gratitude. By handing over the kitchen boy he would, to some extent, be contributing to the shark's traveling expenses. He would be much to blame if, by letting the boy climb into the boat, he should do Manidou out of his rations.

While he still sat hesitating, and wondering how he ought to act, he saw the boy literally jump out of the water with a loud cry, then immediately disappear, and where he had been but a moment before, a shining fin was quivering, turned blood-red by the near-by fire.

The monster had arrived just in time to cut in its fashion the knot of conscience with which, for once in his life, Ti-Coyo had been on the point of getting himself entangled, and the young man felt grateful.

"Ah!" he cried in high good humor, "so there you are! Come over here!"

But the shark, instead of approaching the boat as he had been told to do, began to move slowly in the direction of the wreck, no doubt hoping to come across other kitchen boys no less well nourished.

Ti-Coyo, however, was anxious to be off. He stretched his arm over the side and snapped his fingers, which was his usual manner of summoning Manidou when he was out in his canoe. The shark made a quick turn and hastened toward the boat as soon as he caught sight of the arm that Ti-Coyo was now letting hang down in the water.

Ti-Coyo frowned, looking hard at the fin that was cleaving the surface close beside him. There was something about the shark's behavior which did not seem to him natural. He could not help feeling that the way in which it was moving and behaving (it was Manidou's habit to make a great display of affection after a long absence) was faintly equivocal and unfamiliar.

After all, it was night, and Manidou was not the

only shark streaking through the Caribbean Sea.
Instinctively, he withdrew his arm from under the
very nose of the advancing shark, who had just
reared his head into the air with his mouth open
and his teeth erect. "Why, it's not Manidou at all!"
exclaimed Ti-Coyo, at once startled and angry.

He was filled with indignation that so vulgar a
creature—a shark of obscure birth and inferior social standing, who, now that he came to see him,
close to, was hardly longer than Manidou's tail—
should have had the insolence to take a liking to
him. He might actually have lost an arm!—and he
spat with contempt on the back of the shark, who
made off at once.

He kept his hand upon his knife, still trembling
with fury at the thought of the way in which he
had been insulted. He wanted to jump overboard
and slit the wretched aggressor's stomach, but a moment's reflection convinced him that this was not
the time to choose for engaging in a duel with a
strange shark, so far from St. Pierre, in unfamiliar
waters, and in Manidou's absence. But certainly he
would have brushed all these reasons aside and
yielded to his angry impulse, had he not noticed, just as he was about to dive, that the sea
was crisscrossed with other pointed fins.

The sharks were by no means unaware of what a ship in flames on the high seas meant, and were hurrying up from all directions to be in at the kill.

Two other lifeboats, crammed to their gunwales, emerged at this moment from behind the liner's bows, surrounded by a positive escort—a guard of honor—in the shape of quivering fins. The sharks had got it firmly into their heads that these two heavily loaded craft, so many days distant from any sort of harbor, contained enough eatables and drinkables for all of them. Full of hope, therefore, they stuck to the two boats faithfully.

The *Possenor* was now burning furiously, and the flames, which the light breeze was unable to keep down, were shooting high into the air, and darting their ragged tips in all directions, like beasts of fantasy. Ti-Coyo could hear them panting, complaining, and growling with joy.

They poured from every corner of the ship and out of the portholes, from which the glass had long since burst in fragments as a result of the heat. They flared also from the five or six rows of cabins, one above the other, throughout the whole length of the illuminated vessel, and this produced an impression of festivity.

Whenever, by accident, they touched the water,

there was a brief sizzling noise, and the flames gave the sort of outraged start with which a woman treats a male approach in bad taste, and made off, with necks stretched, in another direction. They fumbled their way over the hull, and ended by making renewed contact with the main body. Not a trace remained of the funnels or the mainmast, or of the bridge or of the after superstructure. The only things still standing were the loading-masts, now red-hot, up and down which little sparks were rapidly darting.

One of the boilers suddenly exploded, and fragments of metal and other things, shot a hundred feet into the air, rained down again at once onto the surface of the sea, which shook with a loud hiss as the blazing mass struck the water, for the ship had taken a sudden list to starboard.

The cooks on the top deck were clinging to the rail and shrieking with terror. They must have been very warm indeed, for the flames were now close to where they were standing. The kitchen boys were faced by the alternative of being eaten by the sharks or burned alive.

If they remained on the ship, they would inevitably be fried like the partridge rissoles they were so adept in preparing; if they jumped overboard, they would be swallowed by the sharks like cheese soufflés—which happened to be one of their specialties. Consequently, their perplexity was extreme. Either alternative seemed to them to be equally detestable, and they begged Ti-Coyo, in the name of Christian charity, to spare them the necessity of making so appalling a choice.

This idea of theirs would have been excellent had they been dealing with anybody else. Only it so happened that Ti-Coyo was of no religion—their own or another—though his son had received he knew not what sort of baptism on an English island. Such an appeal, therefore, was unlikely to make much of an impression on the audience to which it was addressed.

Had Manidou been present at the interview—and present alone at this moment in the sea around the liner—the question would not have been raised, and the fate of the cooks and kitchen boys would have been settled without the possibility of discussion. The nine men in distress would have been adjudged to the monster as his by right, like spoils to a Roman general.

This, however, was not the case. The liner was surrounded by foreign sharks, and Ti-Coyo did not consider it to be his duty to provide food for all the sharks of the Caribbean archipelago. He could not rid himself of the memory that one of them had looked at him with hungry eyes. The recollection of that recent insult did more than all the cooks' appeals or references to some sort of religion to remind him that the lifeboat, after all, was capable of holding fifteen persons at least, and that it would cost him very little to take on board the nine kitchen hands who were by this time squirming in a sheet of flame and stretching their arms to him in supplication.

It was this that decided him to work the boat as close as prudence allowed to the side of the liner, down which the kitchen boys lost no time in dropping a rope ladder.

Ti-Coyo helped the first man into the boat, where he collapsed in sobs. It was the head chef, as was obvious from his high cap and his belly.

In most professions the man of highest rank, when danger threatens, does not consider his own safety until he is sure that those under his orders and in his charge are all safe. In the world of ovens, however, things are arranged differently.

His assistants followed, and Ti-Coyo piled them into the bows, where they sat with chattering teeth, bemoaning their fate. They had had a very close view of death—as close as it is possible to have—

and they attributed their unhoped-for safety to the Lord, with whom they frequently seemed to associate the character of Ti-Coyo—which was too kind on their part. In loud tones they maintained that their feelings of gratitude to both—the Lord, that is, and, incidentally, Ti-Coyo—would end only with their lives.

Ti-Coyo paid not the slightest attention to them. He had spent his childhood in the streets of St. Pierre looking at and listening to the people who loitered there, and there was very little he did not know about gratitude as practiced by the members of the human race. He well knew that the cooks were talking like this only because of the proximity of the burning wreck, and that their gratitude would diminish in direct ratio to the distance of the boat from the fire and the liner.

Ti-Coyo had now once more taken to the oars. With a distinctly unpleasant smile upon his lips he was glancing sideways at the sharks, which, now that the boat was half full, were shadowing her. They very soon broke away, however, and retraced their steps to hang about the ship. No doubt they were of the opinion that their true interests lay in that direction.

All of a sudden, and without uttering a word of warning, the *Possenor* turned turtle. The sea rose up in a great swell and shouted with joy as the flames met it. The long, narrow hull, with its line of red paint, gleamed in the light of the moon, which illuminated the curved and heavy blades of the propeller.

As boots drag a man down in water, so did the stiff, enormous propeller drag the liner to the bottom, slowly and smoothly, until at last it was standing upright in the sea like a standing giant. Then it began to slip deeper, still taking its time. It was as though the sea was swallowing the ship and savoring each mouthful.

Finally nothing remained above the surface but the pointed extremity of the bow, over which, very quietly, the sea's huge, humid mouth closed with a little ripple of white foam, like the saliva at the corners of greedy lips.

A little later the lifeboat was lifted gently on the swell that reached it from the foundered vessel, and rolled silently from side to side in the moonlight.

After first taking careful note of the position in the sky of certain stars with which he was familiar, Ti-Coyo, who had no reason for remaining in this place, unfurled his sail and laid a course for St. Pierre, which he now wanted to reach as soon as possible.

CHAPTER XII

A LIGHT wind was blowing steadily and achieved such wonders with the sail that the boat ran freely before it all through what remained of the night.

Then the sky began to show faintly bright. Ti-Coyo put the tiller hard amidships, and the sun leaped above the horizon like a man suddenly starting from sleep. All the clouds began to blush—apparently from pleasure. At once the air tasted different, and the sea took on a virginal appearance, just as though she had not spent the greater part of the night (as Ti-Coyo could bear witness) in the wildest and most reprehensible activities.

But already the sea had changed her girlish get-up for another dress, and began to drape herself, with astonishing speed, in all sorts of different and full-skirted silks which, as they followed one another, made her look like a completely unfamiliar woman. At one moment, all striped with red and indigo and orange, she seemed a very gypsy; the next, a woman of St. Pierre, swathed in long shawls of vivid green and yellow, and, last change of all (by now the sun had risen a little in the sky), what she really thought she was, a woman of the world, elegant, *soignée,* with just a suspicion of haughty aloofness and enough of affectation to save her from looking stiff and awkward.

Ti-Coyo began to think that, to go to such expense, the sea was surely expecting something: a luxury liner perhaps, or some giant fish. Thereupon Ti-Coyo started unexpectedly to hum, for all beings are moved to sing when the sun rises, as the birds were the first to discover.

At this moment the cooks, from their place in the bow, started to show signs of uneasiness, staring at something in the sea. But it was only Manidou on his way back home, and Ti-Coyo had to make a real effort to keep himself from shouting for joy and caressing the huge, rough back, which was precisely what the creature hoped he would do, as it nuzzled against the boat. But the young man did not want to make an exhibition of himself, and the cooks seemed to be far too much impressed by the size and appearance of Manidou to witness, with any degree of comfort, a demonstration of affection between the shark and the man to whom they had entrusted their safety.

Seeing that Ti-Coyo did not give him even the most ordinary word of welcome, nor make the slightest show of friendship, the shark, who felt thoroughly put out and hurt by such coldness, began to leap ten feet into the air, much to the terror of the kitchen boys, whom he splashed with sea spray from head to foot. It was a trick he had learned from a dolphin who was one of his friends. He produced it now as a way of asking forgiveness for his dilatoriness, and to show how ashamed he felt.

He had made for the open sea at the very first sign of the hurricane, in search of a sheltered spot,

which he had had great difficulty in finding because
he was a stranger to this part of the Caribbean Sea,
and had had to wander all over the place before
happening on a harbor large enough to accommodate a visitor of so vast a size.

As a result, he had been faced by the necessity
of making a pretty long trip in order to catch up
with Ti-Coyo, and it is easy to imagine his anxiety
when he found so many fins at the place where the
Possenor had been only a few hours previously. It
is safe to say that he had lived through some of the
worst moments he had ever known, for, whatever
the degree of love felt by Ti-Coyo for him,
Manidou returned it, with interest. Consequently,
his joy—and relief—when he found his friend again,
was immense, especially when he saw that he was
safe and sound in a solid, seaworthy boat.

Although Ti-Coyo did not address a word to him,
for he could not speak freely to the shark in front
of the kitchen boys, Manidou, who knew him well,
could read from his looks all the anxiety his prolonged absence had caused the young man, and he
felt glad to think that anyone should have been so
upset on his account.

So he indulged in a deal of joyful snorting, and
proceeded to take up a position well ahead of the

boat, with the intention of showing Ti-Coyo the way.

Ti-Coyo had discovered under the seat aft a small cask of drinking-water, as well as some biscuit and bars of chocolate. At noon, therefore, he set about making a parsimonious distribution of these provisions among his passengers.

There was also on board a small compass, which he examined with much curiosity, though, naturally enough, he had no idea what purpose it was intended to serve. He shrugged his shoulders at the notion of anyone needing an instrument to help him find his way through the sea; as though the shark, to say nothing of himself, did not know better than any compass what course they ought to steer.

But the head chef was by no means of this opinion. He looked with great attention at the compass in Ti-Coyo's hand, and pointed out, when the latter set a southerly course, that, according to the compass needle, there could be no possible doubt that the nearest land—and the head chef and his scullions were in a great hurry to reach land of some sort—lay to the north. Ti-Coyo had no intention of discussing nautical matters with anyone of so little consequence as a specialist in the concoction of *rognons sautés sauce madère,* or a champion producer of *haricots au lard,* and set himself to think of other things.

Neither the young man's face nor the look in his eyes encouraged others, as a general rule, to argue with him, and the cook, who had recovered his self-assurance and had, to some extent, forgotten the gratitude that was to end only with his life, turned to his companions in the bow of the boat and began to talk to them in a low and animated tone, without, however, succeeding in making Ti-Coyo pay the slightest attention.

Two hours later a wind rose that made it necessary to shorten sail, since the canvas was jumping all over the place and flapping against the mast. It looked as though it might split at any moment.

Ti-Coyo, who was used to his light and springy canoe, found the boat heavy and slow. She thrust her chin clumsily into the rollers, which were now covering the whole visible extent of the sea and were pressing forward with an appearance of the greatest urgency, one after another, to meet her. Faced by this situation, she flopped heavily back into the troughs, from which she awkwardly emerged, only to fling herself, just as unskillfully as before, at the next wave that turned up under her nose.

Ti-Coyo gazed with wonder at the sea around him. He kept constantly discovering, though he believed that he had always had a profound knowledge of it, something new to look at and admire.

It is a mistake, he thought, to hold, for instance, that all rollers are alike. After watching attentively the way in which they overlapped, jumped on one another's back unexpectedly, and then stretched out voluptuously with grunts of pleasure, Ti-Coyo decided that they were of two sexes. The females swayed their hips, and gave a provocative waggle to their backsides, which were covered in green fabric trimmed with lace, and he could not help thinking that there was something definitely feminine—and lascivious—in the way they were behaving. The male rollers, on the other hand, threw out their chests, thus setting off their upper parts to advantage, and squared their heavy shoulders in their well-fitting dark-gray jackets. They were a rougher and tougher lot.

On this point Ti-Coyo would have liked to hear the shark's views, but Manidou took no interest whatever in such questions, which he judged de-

void of interest, and the young man, who was growing dizzy as a result of staring so long and at such
close range at the game of flying spume and heaving
rollers, began to feel his eyes grow heavy after he
had nibbled at a biscuit and swallowed several
gulps of water.

The kitchen boys were still talking excitedly
among themselves, every now and again turning to
look at the shark in front of them and Ti-Coyo behind. The latter, without being conscious of what
he was doing, finally shut his eyes completely and
fell fast asleep at the tiller, while the boat continued
to toss and flounder over the waves.

A few moments passed, and then Ti-Coyo had a
dream. And in the dream it seemed to him that the
cooks and their assistants in the bows of the boat
got cautiously to their feet and began to creep
stealthily toward him. The head chef was leading
the party, and there was nothing friendly in the
look he fixed on Ti-Coyo, nor did it show a trace
of that gratitude which, as he had solemnly sworn
so short a time before, was to have been eternal.

Ti-Coyo, as he dreamed, had a sense of being in
danger, and he made a violent effort to wake up,
and tried to draw the knife from his belt. But his
hands were encased in lead and refused to obey

him. His body felt so heavy that he could not make the smallest movement, though he was convinced that the least gesture on his part would have been enough to scatter the vermin creeping along beside him, as the flicker of a lash will chase the flies from the eyelids of a dozing animal.

His lips, sealed though they were by the weight of slumber and of nightmare, must have managed to articulate some sound, for the kitchen boys came to a sudden halt, about to turn tail. They appeared to be extremely anxious to make sure that he really was asleep and not just pretending.

When they were completely convinced—convinced that he was sound asleep—they all bent over him at the same moment. Ti-Coyo felt himself seized roughly round the legs, arms, and waist and being lifted up, to be pitched overboard.

Then he woke with a start—under water.

When he struggled to the surface, spluttering and fighting for breath, the shark was beside him. The boat was rapidly vanishing in the direction indicated by the compass. The head chef had taken his place at the tiller, and the kitchen boys were excitedly gazing in Ti-Coyo's direction, as though all agog for something to happen which was being unaccountably delayed.

They were gesticulating wildly, and pointing at him and the shark. He shook his head. It was only too obvious that the head chef and his scullions had wanted so to arrange matters—no doubt in the name of that Christian charity to which they had appealed so loudly on board the burning liner—that Ti-Coyo should meet the same fate that they had been spared, thanks to the intervention of the very person whose continued existence they seemed to find so disappointing. No doubt, too, they were suffering from a sense of grievance at finding that the fin-bearer took such a long time about bringing off his kill. Ti-Coyo was shaking his head because he was angry with himself. "Pity is a bad counselor," the hunchback was fond of saying. He always had a pocketful of proverbs ready to hand.

Because he had momentarily forgotten it, Ti-Coyo was now faced with the prospect of having to swim for several days and nights before he could reach St. Pierre, with a parched mouth and an empty belly, and through weather so rough that he would not be able to get a little rest by floating on his back. He had learned the extent of his powers, and he knew instinctively that he would not be up to facing so heavy a call upon his strength in the state of weakness and fatigue he was in. St.

Pierre was too far away. He would never reach it unaided. Perhaps the best thing would be to go to sleep for good at the bottom of the sea.

Perhaps the shark had already drawn the same conclusions from recent events and could guess what was going on in Ti-Coyo's mind, for he now came close to him, and in the green eyes he fixed on Ti-Coyo were more things than a shark is capable of expressing.

After the passage of each roller, the shark managed, with an engaging air, to manipulate his broad lateral fin into position right under Ti-Coyo's nose. Suddenly, with a little cry, the young man laid hold of it with both hands. Like a flash of lightning, the memory came to him of having seen his scamp of a son being towed in just this way, without fatigue, through the sea.

The shark had been waiting for this to happen, and now set off. He gave Ti-Coyo just enough time to get a firm hold on the welcome fin, to stretch his legs comfortably, and to settle his free arm at his side. After which he started to swim without uttering a word. After all, there was no need to say anything, and Ti-Coyo was certainly in no state to support a conversation. Ti-Coyo knew that even if he fell asleep again during the trip, and loosed his hold on the fin, Manidou would instantly heave to, and find some way of waking him before he dropped off into the water.

The shark seemed to be no less eager than he was to reach St. Pierre, and forged ahead at a speed that even a first-class liner could scarcely have exceeded—but Ti-Coyo had already fallen asleep again, with his hand tightly closed about the fin.

He slept on in this way all through the long night full of flickering lights. The angry rollers lifted him high above the surface of the sea, and flung him from side to side, but this severe shaking did not make him relax his hold, nor did it disturb his slumbers. He dreamed that he was still on board the *Possenor,* which the storm was battering so violently that if he so much as loosed his hold on the brass rail in his cabin, he would find himself on the floor. And so it was that in his dream he clung with all his might to the brass rail, which was, in reality, the shark's fin.

When morning came, the first rays of the sun upon his face awakened him, and the first object that his eyes, still puffy with sleep, took in was a huge column of smoke some distance ahead. He rubbed his eyes, and soon saw that the smoke was issuing from the single funnel of a black-painted freighter flying the British flag. Clearly, those on board had already seen him, for a few moments later they lowered a boat, which rowed toward him at such speed that he barely had time to push the shark away. Manidou was not slow to grasp the nature of this warning, and silently dived under Ti-Coyo's legs. As soon as the boat came alongside, Ti-Coyo clambered on board.

Thirsty though he was, and as hungry as a tiger, he would willingly have dispensed with this piece of good luck. But he saw clearly enough that it would have been difficult for a shipwrecked human in imminent danger of drowning to decline an invitation which was as unexpected as it was generous. For quite obviously that was what the captain of the freighter took him to be—the distressed survivor of a shipwreck alone in the middle of the sea. He had felt it to be his duty, in the name of humanity, to heave to and pick Ti-Coyo out of the water. The young man, however, though he resigned himself to the necessity of laying hold of the rope ladder that was dropped over the freighter's side, felt no gratitude, but silently consigned his rescuer to the devil.

Meanwhile the captain, the first mate, and all the members of the crew, including the engine-room staff, had hurried on deck and were now crowding round him, filled with curiosity.

Ti-Coyo, who was never particularly anxious to tell the truth, now explained that his canoe had overturned, and that he was trying to swim home. The captain shook his head with the air of a man who only half believes what he is being told, and made a sign to one of the men standing by to run to the galley for a bowl of soup, or whatever else might be available. The shipwrecked survivor appeared to be in urgent need of nourishment.

But Ti-Coyo misinterpreted the sign, thinking that it was the captain's intention to keep him by force on his ship until what he had told him could be verified. So he jumped onto the rail and dived into the sea under the very eyes of the astonished crew.

The shark, who had been prowling round the freighter, waiting for his friend, saw him fall and hurried to meet him, just in case of accidents. Ti-Coyo, who was afraid of being followed, dived again, broke surface a little farther off, dived once more, and continued the maneuver, with the shark at his heels, who dived when he dived and rose when he rose, keeping as close to him as though he had been his shadow.

The whole of the crew had rushed to the rail when they saw the young man jump, and hung there, holding their breath when they caught sight of the shark.

"It's a shark of the harmless type," said the captain at last with a sigh of relief; "otherwise the boy wouldn't have got off so lightly. Thirst and exhaustion must have affected his mind. Pick him up again," he concluded, turning to the bosun, "and this time truss him up good!"

Now, the crew consisted entirely of local men— from Barbados, Jamaica, and Grenada—and none of them had ever heard of "harmless sharks," or not, at any rate, in that part of the ocean. Even if such a species did exist—and the bosun didn't really believe it—a monster of the size of the one they had seen swimming beside the shipwrecked man could scarcely be so classified.

The captain, when he turned his head, saw the anxious look on the men's faces, and the expression of apprehension, not to say of fear, in their eyes, for they were making no secret of what they felt.

They were convinced that the youth whom they had picked up was nothing less than one of the "spirits of the deep." The monstrous shark must naturally be his familiar.

The captain gave a shrug. He was quite capable of distinguishing between a "spirit of the deep"— if there really were such beings—and an impudent young half-caste, when he saw one.

But his crew was better informed, with the result that Ti-Coyo was given plenty of time to make off with his shark without being pursued and hoisted on board again, and the captain now resigned himself the more easily to the turn of events seeing that the object of his concern was only a half-caste, after all, as were the sailors who were now refusing to go a second time to his help.

But there was not one of that same crew who did not know, for certain, that when a ship on the high seas, and in the course of a voyage receives a visit from a "spirit of the deep," then, the sooner everyone clears off that ship, the better.

And so it happened that when, a week later, the freighter touched at Colón, every single member of the crew, down to the humblest greaser, made off into the town like a flock of hummingbirds from a clump of guava trees, with the result that it was impossible, later on, to find the least trace of them, and the vessel had to waste three whole days in port in order to recruit a makeshift lot of hands on whom the captain was not at all sure that he could rely.

It was Ti-Coyo who was mainly responsible for the worries that were crowding thick and fast on the commander of the ship, but this was the least of his troubles. He hated to have strangers mixing themselves up in his affairs—he certainly would never mix himself up in theirs—and that was precisely what the captain had done when he had lowered a boat and picked him up. It was only just that he should now be punished. "Pity is a bad counselor." Ti-Coyo had learned that to his cost already, and it was now the captain's turn to have a similar lesson, and he was finding it no less unpleasant.

No, the chief object of Ti-Coyo's concern was not the captain nor his ship—about their misfortunes, incidentally, he knew nothing—but Manidou. For several days now, and several nights, the shark had not been able to take any time off for hunting. He was obsessed by the need to get the exhausted Ti-Coyo back to St. Pierre with the least possible delay, and had quite forgotten about eating. His master, however, who knew what quantities of fish were needed daily to keep Manidou in form, was worrying himself sick.

They had already, more than once, fallen in with shoals of bonito, but the shark had not risked making a detour in order to head them off. He had plugged on toward St. Pierre, which was the sole object of his thoughts.

Ti-Coyo remembered how he had been treated by the cooks and kitchen boys who had owed their lives to him, and who called themselves Christians. He began to wonder, as he clung to the shark's fin, what sort of gods sharks worshipped, and what, in particular, Manidou's religion was like.

When the next night came, and the moon rose, Ti-Coyo uttered a little cry of joy, for he could see in the distance the sharp peaks of Mount Pelée harshly outlined against the sky to his left. Now at last he could breathe easily, and but for the fear that he might leave half his face behind, he would have planted a kiss plumb on the shark's great triangular fin.

That morning Dora had returned from market in a very depressed state of mind, her nose red, her eyes puffy. News of the wreck of the *Possenor* had reached St. Pierre, where it had been the sole subject of conversation since the previous evening. The hunchback saw Lucie's face change color, and though he, too, felt his heart heavy within him, he realized that on this occasion it was his duty to show firmness in the presence of two weeping women.

"What are you afraid of?" said he, speaking in as detached a tone as he could manage, and at the same time executing an impetuous flourish with his crop. "My son's not a chicken to let himself be drowned in a puddle. Besides, the shark's with him."

"That's true," replied Dora, wiping her eyes. "I hadn't thought of that."

Not a further word on the subject was exchanged until dinner-time. Dora laid the table without enthusiasm, knowing well that she wouldn't be able to swallow a morsel, and Lucie was of the same conviction. It so happened that the hunchback, too, for all his pretense that he was not in the least worried, didn't really feel hungry, so that the long and the short of it was that only Guinéo took his accustomed seat.

By chance, spinach figured that day on the menu,
a vegetable for which the boy had no very great
liking, with the result that he felt much inclined,
like his parents, though for a quite different reason,
to go without his dinner. But Dora, with admirable
foresight, had also prepared some of the chocolate
cream that Guinéo adored, and, since he was not
allowed to eat the one without the other—to devour
the chocolate cream without first swallowing the
spinach—mealtimes had become for him something
of a problem.

This evening, however, was different from other
evenings, and it did not take him long to size up
the situation. He saw Lucie sitting in an armchair
staring at nothing, Dora furtively engaged in wiping her eyes, and the hunchback nervously stump-
ing up and down the room with his back turned.
He judged that the occasion was favorable, and the
moment propitious, for a design on which he had
long been brooding.

Without appearing to do so, and moving with
the utmost caution, Guinéo pushed away the plate
of spinach which had been set down under his nose,
and pulled toward him, with no less caution in the
movement, the bowl of chocolate cream. To this he

helped himself once, twice, three times, until
the whole of its contents had descended, in no
time, into his stomach.

Then he made a great show of yawning, having it
in mind to go to bed before his misdeeds should be
discovered. Lucie came out of her brooding fit and
went along, as she did every evening, to tuck him
up. Then she returned to the dining-room, where
the hunchback was still prowling up and down, and
Dora was still blowing her nose, making no noise
and turning her head away.

Somewhere in the house a clock sounded the
twelve strokes of midnight, and Cocoyo announced
that it was time for bed. It would be absurd to sit
up watching, because watching was a thing one did
only when there was someone dead in the house,
and Ti-Coyo was very much alive. Why, at this very
moment, he was almost certainly on his way back
on board some chance vessel that had picked him
up, or swimming in the shark's company. They
could be sure that he might turn up at any
minute.

Having said this, he went with a confident air
toward the staircase that led to the second floor,
where his bedroom was situated. But he had

climbed only the first few steps when the door opened suddenly, and Ti-Coyo appeared on the threshold.

His eyes were red, and he looked worn out and famished.

But this eventuality, too, Dora had foreseen. She had placed on the table, just in case, a plate of cold, underdone roast beef, toward which, without so much as a glance at anybody (he had eyes only for the beef), Ti-Coyo immediately advanced.

Dora had realized that, when he came back—if he did come back—he would be very hungry, and that what he would need would be good red meat —and plenty of it—for the young man, as a result of spending so much time with the shark, had got into the habit of eating only meat—and half-raw meat at that.

It is a way mothers have, to show foresight in matters of this kind. Such care would never have occurred to Lucie, even though for hours and hours she had been thinking only of Ti-Coyo.

"How on earth did you get back?" asked the hunchback in a voice trembling with emotion. He was the first to dare to break the silence.

"When the liner went to the bottom," replied

Ti-Coyo, his mouth full of food, "I thought it was about time for me to go home."

Ti-Coyo added nothing, and the hunchback asked no further questions. He may, perhaps, have felt more worried than either Dora or Lucie, for he felt responsible for what had happened. It had been in order to buy him a sailing ship that Ti-Coyo had set off for Colón on board the liner that had perished by fire on the high seas.

When the four pounds of underdone meat had moved from the plate into his stomach, Ti-Coyo grabbed from the table a glass jug full of water and emptied it to the last drop down his throat. Then he pushed back his chair and tapped the hunchback's protuberance—the front one—an action that brought a happy grin to Cocoyo's face. He knew that the lad would not indulge in such familiarity unless he was feeling on particularly good terms with himself and could think of no other way of giving expression to his satisfaction.

Ti-Coyo next went across to say good-night to Dora, who clung round his neck in tears and blessed him in the names of all the saints. Then he whirled Lucie off her feet, hugged her tightly, and carried her off like a wolf its prey.

Cocoyo watched him going upstairs with Lucie in his arms.

"Blessed if it isn't an abduction!" he muttered, grinning from ear to ear.

"Nobody," murmured Dora with a hint of rather comic yearning in her voice, "has ever carried me off like that!"

"It's never too late!" exclaimed the hunchback with a superb show of bravado, and swaggered across to his wife, whom he tried to lift from the ground as Ti-Coyo had lifted Lucie a moment before.

But either because he had overestimated his strength or because Dora weighed a good deal more than he had expected, all he succeeded in doing was to get their legs all tangled up, with the result that he tripped and measured his length on the floor alongside Dora, whom he pulled down with him in his fall, and whose feet were now madly threshing the air.

"That was no abduction," said Dora with a melancholy sigh, as she helped her husband, who was rubbing the small of his back, to his feet. "That was attempted rape!"

CHAPTER XIII

ALL THROUGH the ensuing months Cocoyo remained as obstinately determined to have a sailing ship as ever Ti-Coyo had been to possess a canoe of his own.

Since the loss of the *Possenor*, when Ti-Coyo had very nearly been drowned through his fault, he had refrained from mentioning the subject. But not a day passed without his getting Guinéo to go into a corner with him and read aloud all the advertise-

189

ments in the nautical journals. When, one day, his grandson told that there was a ship in good condition for sale in the harbor of Fort-de-France, where it could be inspected, Cocoyo, without a word to anybody, and after begging Guinéo to speak of it to no one (he knew that the brat could hold his tongue when he liked), started off that same day for the capital.

"What takes him to town?" muttered Dora, who was eaten up with curiosity.

"Not a word to a soul," whispered Ti-Coyo with an air of deep mystery. "He's off to see a lady of his acquaintance at Fort-de-France!"

Dora burst out laughing, but when Cocoyo got back from the capital that evening, he was puffed up with self-importance. Naturally, both Dora and Lucie wanted to know what was in the wind, but the hunchback eluded all questions, though from the way in which he wriggled his bandy legs it was obvious that he was pleased with himself and with the use he had made of his time.

Dora each day brought back the gossip when she returned from market with her purchases, and next day she informed the whole household that, for the first time since the eruption of Mount Pelée, a ship had anchored in the harbor of St. Pierre, and that the whole population of the place was down on the beach gazing at it in an ecstasy of delight.

"I suppose," she finished up with scorn, though the gleam in her eyes showed that she, too, had been enjoying herself, "I suppose all these people have never seen a sailing ship in their lives!"

"Quite likely," said Ti-Coyo, stretching himself out on the sofa, "because it's a sure thing that that old tub is rotten all through."

The hunchback gave a start that almost brought him out of his armchair. "What d'you know about it?" he asked in a broken voice.

Ti-Coyo, his eyes on the ceiling, explained with a careless air that he had had a fancy that morning to take his canoe and have a look at the sailing ship that was lying at anchor in the harbor. She had been freshly painted, and he had felt a considerable amount of curiosity about what those three fine coats of paint concealed.

That was how he had come to the conclusion that the timber used in her construction must have come straight from the vessel in which Christopher Columbus had sailed when he discovered America, and incidentally Martinique, four hundred years ago. He could think of nothing else that would explain the extreme age of this particular ship, which was rotting where she lay.

Even the mainmast was worm-eaten and would collapse when the first strong wind hit it. Just possibly it might serve as a temporary perch for brainless albatross or by gulls contemplating suicide. As to her bilge, he had counted at least eighteen sizable holes, which had been crudely stuffed with tarred cotton waste, all dripping with sea water. He wouldn't, he added, yawning, and putting a second cushion under his head, take an old sieve like that as a gift, and he felt sincerely sorry for anyone who should be fool enough to go to sea in her.

What Ti-Coyo did not say was that Guinéo had spilled the beans, and that if he had gone to so much trouble to inspect the ship in great detail, the reason was that he had a shrewd suspicion of who the owner was. To make doubly sure, he had gone so far as to put a few discreet questions to the crew, which consisted of three youths recruited in Fort-de-France the day before, whose only experience of the sea, so far, had been gained from the inside of a fishing smack.

They had confirmed his suspicions. The new— they would not go so far as to say happy—owner of the craft was also the owner of a hump on his back, and another on his chest, and he hopped about incessantly on a pair of scurvy legs. One could scarcely go wrong over a description of that kind.

All the time he was talking and describing the state of the vessel, Ti-Coyo could see his father's face contract, and then, as it were, collapse; for the hunchback, who was a miser by nature, had been persuaded to pay three times the value of a ship in good condition for the old tub he had bought on the spur of the moment in Fort-de-France.

By the time his son had finished speaking, Cocoyo was a pitiful sight. The crop had slipped from his relaxed fingers, and his face had turned as yellow as a lemon left on the tree after the July picking. He had fallen back in his chair with trembling lips and haggard eyes. Dora, genuinely alarmed, ran to the kitchen and returned with a bottle of vinegar, which she uncorked and held under his nose, at the same time slapping his cheeks.

"Ah!" murmured Cocoyo in a die-away voice, "I—I—bought—that—ship. She—she belongs to me—to me!"

The hunchback had cheated so many people in the course of his life that he could not bear to think that he had now been cheated in his turn, and cheated like a child. Dora helped him to drag himself to his room, where he at once took to his bed, showing no desire for food of any kind.

The tears welled up in his eyes when he thought of the sum—the enormous sum—that he had had to pay in order to become possessor of this ship of which he had been so proud, only to be assured by his son—whose judgment in such matters was to be trusted—that it was rotten from keel to masthead. He silently cursed the love of mystification and concealment which had led him to act unknown to Ti-Coyo, whose knowledge and competence in everything to do with boats might have saved him from losing so much money that he felt like hanging himself. But even if he did hang himself, as he felt very much like doing, his money would still be in the pocket of that scoundrelly dog who had sold him the worm-eaten old tub.

At this point the hunchback started loudly cursing the whole brood of the boat's former owner, unto the fourth and fifth generation, in such terms that Dora, who was passing her husband's door, beat a hasty retreat. But when a little later, she stopped again to listen, she could hear him moaning and groaning at the top of his voice.

"You didn't handle your father very well," she said to Ti-Coyo next morning, after trying, without success, to make the hunchback, who had refused all food since the previous evening, swallow some soup.

"He's always so secretive," replied the young man with a laugh, "it's time he had a lesson."

"That's true enough," Dora admitted; "but if we don't do something about this ship, we shall be burying him before the week's out."

"Ah!" said Ti-Coyo with a spiteful smile. "I know how to cure him."

"I'd rather be dead than have paid good money for that damned sieve!" groaned the hunchback when he saw his son enter the room.

"That would be a serious error on your part," replied Ti-Coyo quietly, "because that damned sieve, as you call it, is going to bring you a fortune if you know how to go about it. Listen!"

Ti-Coyo had been no more than a youngster, scarcely bigger than Guinéo, a youngster who ran about the street of St. Pierre on the lookout for mischief, when he first heard the story that he now repeated to the hunchback, who had no sooner been made privy to it than he jumped from his bed, put on his shirt the wrong way round, stuffed his tie—

the yellow and red one with green stripes—into his pocket, and went straight off to Fort-de-France. There he proceeded to insure his ship for at least ten times the sum it had ever been worth, even in the far-off days when it had been in a suitable condition to sail the seas.

He also insured a cargo of three hundred casks of rum, all of which, he declared, had come from the last crop of cane gathered on his own plantation. He paid, cash down, to the last farthing the enormous premium demanded, and returned that evening to St. Pierre, where he gave his son an account of his successful mission.

In the course of the next few days, Ti-Coyo and the hunchback employed the whole of their time in filling with water—using hoses for the purpose —the three hundred casks that Cocoyo had sworn to the director of the insurance company were full of a fragrant and high-quality rum.

When all the casks were filled to the brim with the same water that Dora used for washing her dishes, and Lucie for her bath, Cocoyo hired a lighter and loaded them by night onto his sailing vessel, which was lying at anchor out in the harbor. For this purpose he used men from the plantation whose discretion he knew.

Next morning the whole of St. Pierre ran down
to the beach to watch the ship start boldly forth, all
sails set, under the command of Ti-Coyo in person. He had been careful, before leaving, to close
the grille of Manidou's tank, for he did not want
to have the shark dogging his heels at such a time—
because of the three men of the crew whom he
would need later on.

The ship ran before the wind toward the open
sea, and gradually vanished from the eyes of the
numerous watchers, who, overcome with admiration, then dispersed, discoursing on the event.

What a wonderful thing it would be, they agreed,
if other ships decided to follow this one's example,
and came into St. Pierre to anchor, as dozens of
them had used to do years ago, day after day, before
the fatal eruption of Mount Pelée.

By this time the vessel was well out at sea. Ti-
Coyo knew where he was going, and he alone knew.
He gave Dominica a wide berth, and, shortly after
sundown, made certain preparations on board to
which his inexperienced crew paid no attention.

Toward midnight he was waiting until the man
on watch should have dropped off to sleep on a pile
of ropes—something he would never have allowed
in other circumstances—to slip silently into the hold

and worm his way between the casks full of fresh water, after which he made it his business to remove, one after another, the rough-and-ready stuffings that had been poked into the various cracks of the hull.

The sea, which had been on the lookout for something of the sort, began to work its way into the hold, where, less than half an hour later, the casks were afloat and bobbing about delightedly. Ti-Coyo had returned to his cabin, taking the same care not to be seen. There he lay down, fully clothed, on his bunk.

He could feel the hull settling under him. For the past few moments the ship's way had become markedly reduced. He had no intention of being the first to raise the alarm, but rather would wait until one of the members of the watch should realize what was happening, and come with the news to his cabin, where Ti-Coyo would be found simulating deep sleep.

The insurance company would be bound to hold an inquiry into the cause of the wreck, and he was not going to take any chances. He had also foreseen the possibility that the vessel might go to the bottom before any of his imbecile crew understood that anything was wrong—and this was why he

had taken the precaution of keeping the shark confined to his tank.

Manidou would naturally have followed the
ship and its master, and the three young men would
not have had a hope of getting away once the shark
had started to take an interest in the business.

Ti-Coyo felt remorse, of course, at depriving the
shark of a succulent meal at the expense of three
fellows who, as he had not forgotten, had spoken of
the hunchback—his father—in highly disrespectful
terms. No one knew better than he did that Cocoyo
was deformed, but he was inclined to resent having
the fact mentioned aloud in his presence. He certainly would not have arranged to have a solid lifeboat hoisted on board, or to have had Manidou's
grille lowered, had he not needed witnesses who
could be called when, as must inevitably happen,
the insurance company opened an investigation into
the circumstances of the disaster.

Less than an hour had passed when Ti-Coyo
heard the sound of running feet on the deck. A
moment later there came a series of loud thump-
ings on the cabin door, while at the same time
frightened voices cried:

"Captain! . . . Captain! . . . We're sinking! . . .
We're sinking!"

Ti-Coyo took his time about opening the cabin door, and he emerged from it rubbing his eyes and yawning in the most natural manner imaginable. He succeeded in imparting to his features an expression of amazement, which left nothing to be desired, when he leaned over the rail and saw that the ship was so deep in the water that the Plimsoll line was no more than a memory.

The situation was desperate. There was nothing to be done. He ordered the lifeboat to be lowered, therefore, and into it the three members of the crew, all of them not far removed from panic, lost no time in climbing.

As soon as they were some distance from the ship, which was now showing a heavy list, Ti-Coyo stopped the boat. He had it in mind to wait until he had seen with his own eyes the ship and its cargo vanish completely from sight, without leaving a trace on the sea. It needed only one bung to work loose, for a cask, emptied of its contents, no matter what they might be, to bob to the surface, where it might later be discovered.

He wanted, also, to be sure that there was no other ship in the vicinity which, under the pretext of giving assistance to a vessel in distress, might stick its nose in where it was not wanted.

So he waited until the wreck was completely swallowed up, and the sea had ceased to bubble, so as to make sure that nothing—not one of the water-filled casks—had risen to the surface.

Only then did he allow the sailors to bend to the oars.

When news that the ship had foundered reached St. Pierre, it produced a sensation, as was only to be expected, and there were plenty of persons ready to risk making equivocal comments on what had occurred.

There was much speculation also at Fort-de-France where the former owner—who certainly could not guess that the whole affair had been arranged by the hunchback, but merely thought that his old tub had taken the first opportunity of sinking to the bottom of the sea, where she should have been a half century before—swore to whoever would listen that the vessel had been in perfect condition.

It was naturally in the hunchback's interest that he should echo these views, so he, too, swore that the ship had been sound from keel to mainmast, and, furthermore, that the man who had sold it to him had been as honest as the day, though naturally it was Cocoyo's dearest wish that Heaven would one day give him the chance of strangling with his own hands the damned thief who had so shamefully done him out of money about which he could not bring himself to think without the tears starting to his eyes.

Nevertheless, if the hunchback obstinately insisted that he had done a good day's work when he bought the ship, he was merely expressing a great and undeniable truth, for he knew very well what the insurance company would have to pay him as compensation for its loss.

The company, however, was far from satisfied. It could not understand how the ship could have gone to the bottom in just that way, and hurriedly dispatched to the spot half a dozen experts on board a trawler, with instructions to clarify an incident that, to their minds, was wrapped in mystery.

Ti-Coyo and his crew were asked to take these experts to the scene of the wreck. The young man acceded to this request with a very good grace, and allowed the experts conscientiously to examine the whole of that part of the ocean which the three members of the crew, and himself, pointed out to them. But they learned nothing more than they knew already.

Ti-Coyo, as may be supposed, had chosen with very great care the spot in which he intended that the ship should sink. He knew that the wreck was now lying some two or three miles down, well out of range of anybody's curiosity, and certainly of that shown by the experts and their divers, who made their journey and did their diving to no purpose, the more so since Ti-Coyo had taken the trouble—just to be on the safe side—to plump them down a good sixty miles from where the disaster had actually occurred. The members of his crew were so idiotic that they fully bore out his statements, and went so far as to say that they could recognize the place.

The insurance company paid up grudgingly, and the rogue who had sold the ship to the hunchback spent a whole night sobbing when he found out the exact amount of the check that had been sent to Cocoyo—a check that might have come to him if only he had had the gumption to sink his own property—as anybody might have done—after first insuring it for the value of a battle cruiser complete with turrets and torpedo tubes.

When the hunchback had folded the check and stowed it away with infinite precautions, he repeated over and over again the figures written on it. He could not resist the temptation to improvise a mad and extremely curious dance which he executed all over the drawing-room floor. He skidded between the chairs, slid round the whatnots, and twirled about the tables with a cunning intricacy of steps, emitting a series of triumphant howls the while.

"I'm going to buy another rotten ship!" roared Cocoyo at the height of his enthusiasm, dancing more frenziedly. "That pays well!"

"Yes," said Ti-Coyo, "but you can bring a thing like that off once—only."

The hunchback did not share this view, and, anyhow, he was putting far too much energy into his dance to pay attention to what his son was saying.

CHAPTER XIV

It was a year later, as they were sitting over dessert —the occasion was a rather special dinner in honor of the hunchback's birthday—that Lucie decided to bring up a matter that was causing her particular concern.

She had taught Guinéo all she knew, and the child could already read and write, and even count, though not very well. He also had a rough idea of geography, history, botany, and the sol-fa scale. It was time now

—and Lucie expressed this view with great determination—to send him to school.

"What'll he do there?" inquired Cocoyo, pulling
a face expressive of disgust. "If he knows all that
stuff, what more is there for him to learn?"

He had not so much as an inkling of the many
things in which Lucie was extremely anxious to
have her son instructed at school.

"And what school, may I ask?" continued her
father-in-law ironically. "There used to be two or
three of 'em in St. Pierre, and if you like I'll show
you where they stood, and what remains of them
now—just a few crumbling walls and some heaps
of rubble."

"And among the rubble I've noticed quite a few
white bones," put in Dora with an air of detachment, for she thought no more highly of education
or culture than did her husband.

"I hope," he remarked with charity, "that those
bones belonged to the professors who once used to
display in those places their vain and empty knowledge."

"Which, however, and with your permission," retorted Lucie incisively, "I want this child—who happens also to be *mine*—to acquire. There's a good
school," she added, "at Fort-de-France."

The hunchback would not even hear of being separated from his grandson, but he was astute enough to realize that there was nothing to be gained just now by standing up to Lucie. As a rule the young woman was careful to thwart the hunchback's schemes as little as possible, and did her best not to meddle in his concerns. But she had always shown herself to be remarkably obstinate whenever the question of Guinéo's education came up for discussion, and Cocoyo knew that Ti-Coyo, whom he had no intention of opposing directly, would always, if he had to choose between them, take Lucie's side.

Now, therefore, he hastily changed his tactics. He was getting on, he said with an assumed air of melancholy, and felt that the little strength remaining to him was dwindling with each day that passed. Wouldn't it be a terrible thing for him if, one of these days, he had to pack up his traps for good and all, and die without one farewell look at the grandson whom they were planning to send away? He had always hoped that the boy would be at his bedside to help him when he breathed his last.

These words he accompanied with a sigh which gave his listeners a pretty good idea of what that last breath would be like, so much conviction and

power did he put into it—power that did honor to
the lungs of a man so near his end.

Dora turned away her head so that her smile
should not be seen. She was certainly not unaware
that he had never been more brisk than now, so
brisk, indeed, that he never gave the wretched men
who were employed in weeding the plantation a
moment's peace. They were more afraid of him
than of any hurricane, and whenever they saw him
suddenly appear, crop in hand, among the tall sugar-
canes, they crossed themselves and silently called
upon the Lord for help.

Cocoyo saw Dora's smile, but it did not prevent
him from indulging still more in self-pity. It would
be a crime, he said, to separate him from Guinéo.
What, he asked, had he ever done to deserve such
cruel treatment from Lucie? Had she, he whim-
pered, no feelings of pity?

Ti-Coyo slipped unobtrusively from the room
in order to have a good laugh on the veranda, where
the others could not see him. This was the first
occasion, so far as he knew, that Cocoyo had ever
referred to pity without immediately adding that
it was a "bad counselor," which was true enough,
as he had learned only too well in his dealings with
the sea cooks.

On his return to the dining-room he found Dora, who was no doubt anxious to draw a curtain over the memory of her smile at the hunchback's words, making great play with her handkerchief which she was using to wipe from her eyes some tears that had never been shed.

Lucie was not in the least taken in, but she did not want to make matters worse, though she took her father-in-law's facial contortions no more seriously than she did Dora's tears. She therefore suggested that a tutor should be engaged.

At these words Dora sat up very straight and declared, with a hideous squint, that she wasn't going to have any strangers in her house.

"All right, then," said the hunchback, who knew that he could never hope to get the better of Lucie on a subject of this kind, and thought that this might be the best solution, "the tutor can live at the hotel. I don't see," he added with a cruel glint in his eye, "why he shouldn't rent the room where that South African was exposed to the 'spirits of the river.' He can come here during the daytime to take charge of the boy."

This proposal met with general approval, and Lucie wrote that very same day to relations of hers at Fort-de-France asking them to help her to find what she wanted—a fine man, with not much native blood in his veins, whose curly mustache and solemn bearing immediately aroused feelings of dislike in both Guinéo and his grandfather—for different reasons, but equally deep.

"He's a damned prig!" said Cocoyo after a single glance at the new tutor.

"He is a Master of Arts," retorted Lucie, "and will teach my son Latin."

"Do you want to make a priest of him, then?" asked the hunchback with surprise, for it had never occurred to him that Latin could be of any use except for saying Mass.

Lucie shrugged her shoulders, and the tutor took up his duties forthwith.

Guinéo, who had inherited, along with other family virtues, his father's cunning and his grandfather's powers of dissimulation, was careful not to let his tutor see the dislike he inspired in him. On the contrary, he was at pains to be as obedient and as friendly as possible.

He managed to keep this up so long as it was merely a question of imparisyllabics, and Guinéo carried his good nature so far as to endure a number of rather tedious explanations—or that was how they seemed to him—on the subject of the ablative absolute. He went even further and allowed the different uses of the gerund in certain circumstances to be mentioned in his presence. But when, after a year, the tutor confronted him with the deponent, and even the semi-deponent, verbs, it was borne in on Guinéo that the time had come to put an end to these subversive activities, and to execute the plan he had been keeping up his sleeve for just such a situation.

Pedant though he might be, the tutor was a decent enough fellow, though to some extent lacking in astuteness, and he set himself to grapple conscientiously with the urchin, to whom he had become attached, and whose affection he quite honestly believed he had won.

From the very beginning Guinéo had done everything in his power to encourage this very erroneous conviction. Furthermore, with his large, innocent, and shining eyes, his delicate features, his dancing curls, and that trustful smile which even the shark had been unable to resist, he could, when he set his mind to it, win over almost anybody—as he very well knew. He knew, too, how to make use of this arsenal of weapons—expression, smile, and the rest—with a grace and a mastery which Célimène herself could not have surpassed or even equaled.

It had therefore been the easiest thing in the world for him to gain, from the very first moment, the affection of a Master of Arts as frank and open-hearted as was the tutor.

Since, too, this same tutor showed, whenever the opportunity served, the greatest deference to Dora, whose handkerchiefs thrilled him, whose massive gold ornaments impressed him, she ended by half forgiving him for being what he was—a tutor—and was won over to the cause of education. She even went so far as to persuade the hunchback to invite to Sunday lunch the man whom he still regarded as a prig and a fop.

Their guest made it quite clear that he was overcome by the luxury of his hosts' establishment, and the fierce and ironical expression of the hunchback's face had the effect of so completely reducing him to silence that he scarcely opened his mouth during the meal except to eat, and made no attempt to display his learning, which he would most gladly have done in any other company.

It had become his custom, early each afternoon, to take Guinéo by the hand and walk with him through the streets of St. Pierre. The boy, needless to say, took very little pleasure in these expeditions

with such a companion, but Lucie approved
of them, and so he could not avoid them.

The ruins with which the town was still encumbered, furnished a hundred opportunities for medi-
tation and disquisition, and the tutor drew from
them lessons designed to instruct a young mind in
wisdom.

"When we lost St. Pierre," he exclaimed emphat-
ically, coming to a halt on a pile of rubble and
raising his eyes to heaven, "we lost everything!
What would France be cut off from Paris and her
élite?"

Guinéo could not say, and did not care. He
amused himself with picking up here and there
glass bottles which the heat of the eruption had
twisted, as a laundress twists washing, and which
Dora was forever throwing away when he took
them home.

The tutor had managed to get hold of a plan of
the city as it had been formerly, and took pleasure,
as they walked, in assigning to its former site each
heap of ruins that they passed, and in adorning his
remarks with Greek and Latin quotations taken
from the best authors.

In this way, with melancholy gusto, he drew

Guinéo's attention—the boy's mind was elsewhere—
to the remains of the Law School, once the haunt of
the legitimate and illegitimate, half-breed and other
sons of the creole nobility; of the Grand Théâtre,
where performances used to be given all through
the year by the best comedians and singers from
Paris, engaged at enormous expense; and of the ter-
race in front of the Casino, where not a day had
passed without fights and public assassinations being staged by the hot-blooded and proud half-castes,
who once had fought side by side with the white
planters against the abolition of slavery in 1789,
and who were known in France as the "gentlemen
of Martinique."

Up to the time of the eruption of Mount Pelée,
dueling had been a favorite form of amusement in
this ancient city, where swords were drawn for the
silliest of reasons—especially when the honor of her
women was concerned—and frequently for no reason at all, for these "gentlemen of Martinique" had
a passion for cold steel, and were extremely touchy
in the matter of honor, which they routed out
everywhere, and often in places where it had no
business to be. Also, they had it in mind to make
good their reputation as some of the best swords-
men in the world. But, sighed the tutor, where

were they now? And where were all those others
who had been the glory of this town and of this
island?

Whereupon the tutor would punctuate his per-
oration with several of those profound aphorisms
for which Anaxagoras, Heraclitus, and other ornaments of the Ionian school had been responsible,
before continuing his pious and ardent pilgrimage.

Opposite the ruins of a celebrated house where,
behind drawn blinds, had once lived absolutely rav-
ishing young women, whose intimacy anybody
could enjoy on the condition of first disbursing a
considerable sum of money to a middle-aged lady
of venerable appearance, the tutor called a halt to
declaim in Latin a passage from Tibullus, who had
maintained, in verse, that it was necessary only to
make love to enjoy the favor—if one might so put
it—of the gods.

The tutor was well aware that the boy, most for-
tunately, could not guess the reason for such profane transports inspired by a building which had
been profane in more than one sense, but he nevertheless made an attempt to justify them to his pupil,
and felt little or no embarrassment in finding—
always in Latin, and in verse—an adequate excuse
for his enthusiasm.

"All men take their pleasure as it comes," he translated with an indulgent smile. "*Trahit quemque sus vo . . .*"

"Naturally," interrupted Guinéo with a bored smile, for he found no amusement in Latin, and took his own pleasure in the society of the shark and not of the tutor.

Sometimes the latter would direct his steps, and those of his charge, to the seashore, where he paid a moving tribute to the boats filled with flowers, hung with multicolored lanterns, and propelled by guitar-playing boatmen, which, in the old days, through the long, warm nights, had carried embracing lovers across the harbor, and in which, as they were rowed onwards, many things had happened.

After these expeditions he would set about explaining to Guinéo, with a deep sigh (those times were no more!) and an important-sounding cough, though the digression was now of very little interest, how, many centuries ago, a catastrophe had cut the American continent in two and had caused to arise in the sea between the dissevered parts that multitude of islands which form the Caribbean archipelago, of which Martinique happens to be the most glittering ornament.

Guinéo pretended to be listening with attention,

though in reality his mind was occupied with matters differently fascinating, like, for instance, trying to find out whether the shark would take as short a time to swallow the tutor (assuming that the opportunity was given him by some kindly disposed and skillful person) as he had done to ingurgitate Cric, the little dog.

CHAPTER XV

A DAY CAME when the tutor decided that the time had come to add the dry-as-dust passive verbs to the difficulties with which Guinéo was already wrestling in the matter of the deponent and semi-deponent ones. The boy thereupon made up his mind that his cup was full, and that there was no point—this he saw clearly—in humoring any further a man who seemed to have no idea in his head beyond raising new causes of trouble between him and

Lucie, who had already become far too persistent in her attempts to find out the progress made by her son in the language of Cæsar.

When, therefore, at the end of Sunday luncheon, the tutor once again took his pupil by the hand, Guinéo insisted on taking the path to the beach. No sooner had they reached it than he suggested that, after so much walking about the ruins, it would be a good thing to go for a row.

But perhaps, he added quickly, when he noticed the tutor's forehead contract in a frown, he did not know how to swim. For he had not lived with the hunchback for nothing, and had acquired a good deal of information touching the nature, and the weaknesses, of human beings. No doubt, he said, the tutor might be afraid of venturing far out in a boat, and quite possibly he had never learned how to use a pair of oars.

These three suggestions were calculated to wound the pride of any native of Martinique, and the tutor's hackles rose immediately—as Guinéo had guessed they would—at hearing such insulting doubts expressed by his young charge.

He was, he said, proudly drawing himself to his full height, a native of Martinique, having been born in the commune of Les Trois-Ilets, which had given to France an empress, to whom, indeed, he was in some sense related (one of his ancestors had been housekeeper in the Tascher de la Pagerie family), and as familiar with the sea as any Scandinavian could be with the snow. As to boats, their sails, their gear, and their oars, he could assert without fear of contradiction that they had been his earliest playthings—playthings of which he had never grown tired, and in which, all his life long, he had found a source of amusement and delighted wonder.

Saying which, since he desired, without further delay, to provide Guinéo—who had hoped all along that that was what he would do—with incontrovertible proof of what he had just announced, he raised his eyes and scanned the beach for sight of a boat to hire.

That, too, Guinéo had foreseen, and he at once directed his tutor to Robert Fil de Fer, who was busy mending his nets at no very great distance.

Now, not long ago Robert Fil de Fer had made the mistake of causing Guinéo to pay more for his fish than it was worth, and the boy had ever since nursed the intention of one day settling accounts with him.

What he now had in mind was to kill two birds

with one stone—to get rid of his tutor and at the same time revenge himself upon the fisherman. Co-coyo was never tired of saying, day in and day out, that a debt, whether recent or of long standing, is still a debt, and that a man should always take the first chance that offered of paying what he owed, whether the obligation dated from the immediate past or was so old that the creditor barely remem-bered it, or, as was the case with Robert Fil de Fer, had forgotten it altogether.

That chance, thought Guinéo, had now come. The hunchback's words had not fallen on deaf ears.

For reasons that he alone could fully appreciate, he judged that the present moment was altogether favorable for the execution of his double plan. Everything, including the tutor's indignant reaction to the boy's treacherous insinuations in the matter of his knowledge of the sea and its craft, seemed to conspire to provide just the opportunity he needed —too long delayed—in order to give proof of the gratitude he owed to Robert Fil de Fer.

A price was agreed upon, and the tutor, with an air of easy nonchalance, started to push the boat down the sand. Just as he was about to embark, he drew himself up, and poetically called Lucretius to witness—as though he knew what was about to happen:

"*Suave mari mag . . .*"

But he was roughly interrupted by Guinéo. "Let's get going," said the boy. He had not made a study of Lucretius, and was in a hurry to get done with the business in hand.

Instead of waiting until he should be told where to sit, he took up a position in the bows, from where, as he explained with one of his most charming smiles, he would be able to keep a keen lookout ahead.

The truth of the matter is that he had good reasons—which concerned nobody but him—for being behind the tutor, who, absorbed in his rowing, would have to turn his head should he wish to say anything to his pupil.

The boy was far from ignorant of the fact that, just under where he was sitting, there was a large cork that effectively closed a hole in the boat's bottom. He could feel it with his foot, and the contact made him tremble with pleasure. It was the presence of this cork that had made it necessary for him to sit precisely where he had elected to sit, and nowhere else.

The tutor now unbuttoned his collar and loosened his tie so that he might breathe freely. This done, he bent to the oars with a will. He was eager to show Guinéo—who, he felt, had not seemed genuinely convinced by his assertions—what he could accomplish once he had got a pair of oars in his hands, and a craft light to maneuver beneath his feet.

Guinéo, for his part, leaned well forward, shielding his eyes from the sun, the better to scrutinize the sea. He seemed to be looking for something—or somebody.

When the boat had reached a point a good half a mile from the shore, and Guinéo had examined the roadstead with not a little impatience without finding what he was looking for, he cupped his hands about his mouth with a determined air and gave a full-throated cry:

"Manidou! . . . Ho! . . . Manidou!"

"What's that?" asked the tutor, turning his head. "Whom are you calling?"

"Nobody," replied the boy coolly. "That's just a noise I make when I am happy. The sea always has that effect on me."

Whereupon he cupped his mouth again and shouted at the top of his voice: "Manidou! . . . Ho! . . . Manidou!"

If the shark was in the neighborhood and failed to heed the summons, the reason was that he was— no denying it—as deaf as a post.

The tutor returned to his rowing. His face showed a simple-minded smile occasioned by the sheer happiness, the emotional exaltation, of his young charge, who had just resumed his joyful shouting when he saw the object he was calling not, as he had expected, at some considerable distance, but close against the boat.

Guinéo leaned out and reached his hand to stroke the back of his recently arrived friend, when the tutor turned his head to tell him to keep quiet and not to put his hand in the water, because he had been told that the harbor was alive with sharks.

"That's just a legend," replied the boy gaily, caressing the great fin that was within easy reach of his hand. "You mustn't believe everything you hear."

With these words he leaned down to raise from under his feet the big cork that stopped up the hole in the bottom of the boat, which fishermen take out when they want to run off the water they have shipped, when they have hauled their craft up on the sand.

The cork jumped out, and the sea at once rushed joyously into the hole.

Guinéo began to whistle through his teeth. He was extremely curious to see what would happen next—events that he had set in motion.

"Here, I say!" exclaimed the tutor ten minutes later, realizing that he was ankle-deep in water. "We're shipping water!"

"Yes," said Guinéo with a fine carelessness; "there's probably a loose board in this rotten old tub. But it's not far from the shore, and we'd better swim for it. You did say," he added with no less ferocity than the hunchback would have shown in similar circumstances,"you did say you could swim."

"Of course, of course," replied the tutor with no enthusiasm. He was fully dressed, and was thinking what the fine suit he was wearing—his Sunday suit— had cost. "But can't we stop up the hole?"

And the tutor, abandoning the oars, stood up with his handkerchief in his hand, intending to use it to stuff into the hole when he had found it. But he had waited too long, and it was now too late. The boat, half-filled with water, was already sinking beneath him, and Guinéo, without delaying further, jumped lightly overboard and began to swim, close by the shark, into whose ear he whispered:

"See what a lovely meal I've arranged for you!"

But Manidou knew nothing about that. So far he had not noticed the tutor. Still, he was only too willing to believe the boy, and gave a little wriggle just to show that he was full of hope and anticipatory gratitude.

The boat slid away from under the tutor's feet while he was trying, without success, to rid himself of his clothes. The shark, who had only partially grasped Guinéo's meaning, understood its full significance when he found himself suddenly confronted, only a few yards away, by this fat and healthy male splashing about in the sea—the sort of male for whom he had a passion. Without further ado, he made straight for him.

At this very moment the tutor turned round in the water to instruct his pupil to make for the shore as quickly as possible, adding that, if he got tired, he had better put his arms round his neck. But scarcely were the words out of his mouth when he caught sight of the fin cleaving the surface and coming in his direction.

Guinéo saw the poor man's eyes dilate with horror, and heard his shriek, for the shark had just snapped at his legs. His mouth was twisted, his

face convulsed, and he had barely time to emit a
gurgling noise (perhaps he was trying to address
the words *"Tu quoque!"* to the boy) before rejoining his legs in the shark's belly. Nothing was
left on the surface but a couple of pink and greasy
circles on the spot where, a moment before, a fine
figure of a man—the unofficial relative of an empress
of France, with a brain chock-full of the linked
beauties of Greek and Latin—had been flounder-
ing.

"You didn't finish him off as quickly as you did
my poor Cric," said Guinéo reproachfully to the
shark, who had swung round quickly to meet him.

The monster was lashing the sea with his great
tail. He was in no hurry, because he felt happy and
wanted Guinéo to know it. All his life long the tutor had done nothing but brain-work, and this fact
had imparted to his flesh a peculiar tenderness and
a flavor which were very much to the shark's liking. The fishermen of St. Pierre, trained to hard
physical labor, and nourished on coarse food, could
offer nothing like it.

Manidou would have liked to clear himself of the
reproach that he had been slower about eating the
tutor than the dog. But the two morsels had nothing
in common. One had been large and deliciously

fat, whereas the other—the little dog—had consisted
of nothing but bone and hair. No comparison was
possible. Guinéo should have realized that, and
Manidou could not but feel that he had been un-
justly criticized.

He was just about to explain this in his own way,
when the boy gave him a sharp push, which meant
that he had better get out of sight. Ti-Coyo had
long ago trained him to obey this signal, and he
dived immediately into deep water. He had enough
wit and tact to understand that it was better, when
he had just swallowed a man, to make himself
scarce as soon as other men—this time in boats—put
in an appearance.

The fishermen had seen the boat sinking from
the shore, where they were busy with their own concerns, though, naturally enough, they knew nothing
of the part played by the shark. They now hurriedly
set about taking help to the wrecked occupants of
the boat.

"Where's the man who was with you?" they asked
the boy when they had hoisted him, dripping with
water, into a boat.

"He was drowned," replied Guinéo in his most
engaging manner. "He didn't know how to swim."

The fishermen shook their heads with an air of

incredulity. The idea that there could be anywhere in the world a man incapable of propelling himself in salt water was quite beyond their comprehension, especially when this man had been born in their island. They had, however, to rest content with this explanation, and rowed back to the shore at top speed, after first carefully inspecting the sea around them.

Guinéo felt thoroughly contented—more contented than he dared to show—when, on reaching land, he saw Robert Fil de Fer dancing about on the sand in an access of despair. The man was noisily lamenting the loss of his boat and waving his arms in a frenzy. In the space of a few minutes he had lost the means of his livelihood, which he had bought after years of skimping and privation.

Guinéo knew this, which was why his little heart was overflowing with happiness. Here was a very different Robert Fil de Fer from the man who, in the old days, had, with impunity, tacked on six sous to the price of every pound of fish he had sold him. He had got his reward now, right enough! "Such a lovely boat, too!" wailed Robert Fil de Fer, rolling his eyes, "and in perfect condition! I don't see how it could have sunk!"

Nor did anybody else, except Guinéo, who was

now running gaily toward the house of his parents. To them, in his own fashion, he described the accident. He assured them that it was the tutor who had insisted on the expedition. He himself had not been very keen, because he did not want to have anything to do with Robert Fil de Fer, whom he knew to be a thief.

Ti-Coyo listened to the story with concentrated attention. He knew that the boy was as capable as he was himself of harboring a grievance, and that Guinéo was not more likely to have forgotten the debt that he believed himself to have incurred than he, Ti-Coyo, would have felt inclined to expunge from his memory what, years ago, he had owed to another fisherman—Nat the Mulatto.

But he knew also, from having traveled in it when he made his trip to Fort-de-France, that the boat was a new one, and that Robert Fil de Fer was in the habit of looking after it with the greatest care. It seemed, therefore, strange to him that it should have sunk for no apparent reason, in fine weather, less than a mile from land.

"Wasn't there any other boat on the beach for hire?" he asked.

There had been dozens of them neatly drawn up on the sand. But chance had so ordered matters—

pure chance—that the tutor should pick out that one—that of Robert Fil de Fer—from all the rest. Its fine appearance had attracted him from the first moment he set eyes upon it.

That, at least, was what Guinéo said with conviction, fluttering his eyelashes. Ti-Coyo scratched his head.

"So," he said, winding up the conversation, "this chap, your teacher, got drowned because he didn't know how to swim?"

"Yes," said Guinéo, with a further flutter.

Now, Ti-Coyo remembered clearly having seen this same tutor—who had been drowned because he did not know how to swim—frequently diving into the Roxelane and doing the overarm stroke just where the river was deep enough to make it possible for anyone to drown who had had a mind to, and he could not help wondering how the fellow had managed to sink like a stone when he was no more than ten minutes from the beach.

Nor had he forgotten that the grille of the tank had been raised ever since morning, and the shark given complete liberty to reach the open sea. Manidou, however, had returned home a quarter of an hour before—in order to digest his meal in peace.

After a little further thought, and without a word

to anybody, Ti-Coyo went down the path to the tank, which, after first taking off his clothes, he entered, and proceeded to force open Manidou's mouth. While this was happening, the monster looked at him with eyes as innocent as Guinéo's had been a little while before.

Ti-Coyo knew, however, how much, or how little, a shark's expression can mean, and he set to work feeling about in the creature's gullet.

Now, a shark's teeth are saw-pointed and curved. When their owner is resting they remain retracted. He has no toothpick and, even if he were given one, would not dream of using it. That is why it is always possible to find in his throat, or caught between his teeth, the remains of his last meal, and often of earlier meals as well.

Ti-Coyo found what he was looking for at a point halfway between Manidou's throat and stomach. He managed to reach it by thrusting his arm up to the shoulder into the monster's mouth. By this means he succeeded in bringing to the light of day a scrap of something that he examined with interest as he walked back up the path.

There had also been, in the same spot, a mass of other things, which he had preferred not to touch.

The hunchback came out to meet his son, whom

he had seen, a few minutes earlier, moving so unobtrusively away. He, too, looked very carefully at what Ti-Coyo was carrying in his hands.

"Hm!" he said at last; "a nice piece of tweed. I noticed at lunch that the tutor was wearing a very well-cut suit of just that material. Where did you find it?"

"In Manidou's throat," replied Ti-Coyo briefly.

Cocoyo emitted a little whistle, which one could interpret as one liked, and then kept silent a moment. A couple of wood-pigeons had just alighted almost at the feet of the hunchback, who now began to laugh, for he had just remembered that the tutor had been in the habit of carrying in his waistcoat pocket a large old-fashioned watch of chased silver, the double case of which contained a remarkably musical chime.

"It's quite likely," he exclaimed between his guffaws (he found the whole thing so comic, and laughed so heartily, that he was attacked by a fit of hiccups, while the tears streamed from his eyes), "it's quite likely that the chime is sounding the hours in the shark's stomach!"

Ti-Coyo gave his father a nasty scowl. He found him rather too much inclined to treat with indulgence the many stupid things that Guinéo frequently did. He replied, therefore, with a somewhat evil glint in his eye:

"You can find out easily enough whether that is so. You've only got to get into the tank and stick your ear against the shark's side."

He thought that he had caught the hunchback out good and proper, but Cocoyo was not the kind of man to be trapped so easily. He blandly repudiated the suggestion.

"Why should I?" he said. "That would do no good. I'm deaf in both ears, and if Manidou had swallowed a cathedral chime, I shouldn't hear it."

This was the first time that Ti-Coyo had heard of his father's deafness, and he said nothing. But just as the hunchback was waddling away, he took a golden louis from his pocket and dropped it on the pebbly path, where it rolled with a pleasant chinking sound. Instinctively Cocoyo swung round and dashed, with hands outstretched, toward the piece of money which was shining a few feet from him. But he brought himself up sharp, with some confusion, before he had reached it, because he noticed that his son was watching him with an ironic expression on his face. He straightened his back and put his hand to his ear as though he were listening attentively to some distant sound. Then he said:

"I am not quite so deaf as I thought, because I could have sworn I heard, from where I'm standing, that chime in the shark's stomach. But it was only," he added, "the sound of this coin that had slipped out of my pocket."

Saying which, he bent down, picked up Ti-Coyo's gold piece, and coolly put it in his pocket. Then he waddled away with colors flying.

"It's all most unfortunate," said Lucie some time later. "Now I shall have to find another tutor for the boy."

Needless to say, Lucie had not the slightest suspicion of what had really happened, and accepted the story of the regrettable accident in perfect good faith. But Dora knew differently.

"Oh well," she said with a slight shrug, "I don't suppose he'd have lived to make old bones."

CHAPTER XVI

One AFTERNOON the new parish priest of St. Pierre
(his predecessor had been buried under the ruins
of his church, thanks to the benevolent activities
of Mount Pelée) started off on foot for the plantation.

He was very eager to have at least a decent chapel
built on the site of one of the vanished cathedrals.
But no matter how hard he begged, no matter

how far he walked, nor how many visits he made
to his parishioners, the money was coming in far
more slowly than he could have wished—and than
was necessary if the work were to proceed satisfac-
torily.

The people he approached with his requests com-
plained at greath length of the difficult times. Business, they said, was at a standstill, while the prices of
everything needed for the nourishment of human
beings, and of even the most elementary comforts,
were shooting up.

In short, money was scarce (St. Pierre, alas, was
not what it had been!) and perhaps, said they, the
priest would be well advised to wait a bit before
going ahead with his chapel.

The rough wooden building in which he said his
daily Mass was, there could be no denying, un-
worthy of the Lord. It was the Lord, however, who
had taken it light-heartedly upon Himself to reduce
to rubble the magnificent cathedrals that generations
of men had worked hard to raise to His glory. It
was hard not to feel bitter when one remembered
that glorious Ascension Thursday when three or
four bishops, assisted by dozens and dozens of arch-
deacons and deacons, had solemnly celebrated, to
the sound of the great organs of both cathedrals,

packed to bursting with the faithful, those moving
ceremonies which Mount Pelée had brought so
brutally to an end, in the space of a few minutes.
The Lord really had only Himself to blame if His
servant—the priest—had now been reduced to the
position of a mere official who had to carry out his
functions in the most squalid of settings.

Besides, all that really mattered, surely, was that
Masses should be said—as they were—even if only
in a wooden shanty. God is everywhere, and it was
not very likely that He would take offense at such a
state of affairs. He must know better than anybody
else how difficult life had become in a city for
which, so recently, He had shown such marked concern—as Mount Pelée was there to witness.

The priest had grown used to hearing talk of
this kind from people who were in no hurry to give,
even to their Creator, the money which, according
to them—and it may have been true—they had
found it so hard to come by. And so it was that,
in despair, he had decided to visit the hunchback,
who was the richest man in St. Pierre.

He knew that in Cocoyo's house he had at least
one excellent parishioner, for each Sunday he saw
Lucie in the front row of seats in his wooden shanty,
following the Mass with deep devotion.

He felt less sure that the hunchback and his son were equally ardent Christians. The best thing he could do, therefore, was to go in person and see how the land lay, and this he made up his mind to do.

The first person he saw on reaching the house was Cocoyo, whose greeting was not exactly enthusiastic. He changed color when he heard the reason for the priest's coming, for though he was now well provided for, he showed no inclination to throw his money out of the window, as Guinéo had more than once had occasion to notice.

Besides, the hunchback tended to lump together Education and Church, tutors and priests, for none of which could he see any use in this world. Consequently, it was no part of his intention to be parted from any fraction of his fortune, no matter how small—not even from the gold louis out of which he had so cleverly, and so recently, cheated his son —for the benefit of the priest and his chapel; still less in honor of a God to whom he owed precious little gratitude for the manner of his birth.

All the same, he was careful not to put these thoughts into words. His idea was to settle accounts with the priest—and none knew better how to settle accounts—by paying a few fulsome compliments, because he knew that Lucie would take it very ill should he show himself ill-mannered or insolent toward a member of the Catholic clergy.

Dora entertained no more friendly feelings than her hunchbacked husband did for the Lord or for His servitors on this planet, and for the same reasons, reasons of a purely physiological description; and she looked glum when Lucie suggested that they ought to invite the priest to stay to dinner.

Nevertheless, both of them—the hunchback and Dora—could keep a stiff upper lip when faced by misfortune. Dora even went so far as to prove once again how truly she deserved her reputation as a *cordon bleu* which was generally recognized by all and sundry—not excepting Guinéo, when spinach did not figure on the menu. She therefore busied herself to good effect among her pots and casseroles, which were soon dancing gaily on the kitchen range.

Faced by such reckless activity, Cocoyo could scarcely do less than produce, from the secret hiding-place where he kept it safe from prying eyes, a bottle of his best rum—a rum so superexcellent that the Governor of Martinique himself might count it fortunate if he got a taste of it more than three times in the whole course of his career—and this the hunchback now placed reverently on the table.

Lucie was delighted, and everything went as well as possible—at least, until the moment for dessert arrived.

It so happened that the priest was deeply appreciative of good food, for, said he, he liked nothing better than to honor the life that his Creator had given him. He knew how to do justice to good food, especially when there was a noble bottle with which to wash it down.

Therefore, when Lucie had promised to contribute a sum (the size of which, when he heard it, made Cocoyo pull a terrible face) toward the building of the chapel, the priest threw himself back in his chair—his digestion working smoothly, and his nose buried in his glass—and expressed some surprise that he had never yet seen Guinéo at the rectory.

The boy gave the priest a nasty look, and the hunchback pursed up his lips.

"He might get mixed up with a bad lot," he observed dryly. "All the scapegoats of St. Pierre use it as a meeting-place. They might be a shocking example to him and teach him evil ways."

"Yes," said Dora, backing him up, and squinting in the strangest fashion. "They might, for example, teach him to steal."

Ti-Coyo hid his face in his napkin so that their guest should not see his smile. Guinéo had never needed anyone to teach him how to steal—not even his own parents.

The priest, not unnaturally, expressed indignation at such a charge, and warmly asserted that all the young people who came to the rectory were strictly honest. He always made sure of that before allowing them into the house of God.

Dora chose this moment to set upon the table a rice cake with rum sauce, flavored with vanilla, and sprinkled with nutmeg, cinnamon, and ginger. The sight of it at once put an end to the discussion. For the next few minutes everybody was so busy doing justice to this succulent dessert that not a word was spoken around the table.

When, at last, the conversation was resumed, the incident had been entirely forgotten, even by the priest, who declared with an air of benevolence, with which no doubt the rice cake had something to do, that since the day when he had said his first Mass, he had visited many homes, but never one where the inhabitants seemed so happy, so united, so deserving of the highest esteem, as here—and he gave thanks to Heaven in French and Latin.

At this point Dora was seized with a fit of cough-

ing, and her eyes, bright with happiness, seemed to
be turning in every direction at once. "You haven't
seen Uncle Manidou yet," she said.

Cocoyo bounced out of his chair, and very nearly
choked over the rum that he was engaged in sip-
ping.

"And who, may I ask," inquired the priest in his
most courteous voice, "is Uncle Manidou?"

"He's the best of the bunch!" replied the hunchback without a moment's hesitation, having recovered his self-control. In saying this he was, perhaps,
not so very far from the truth.

"A being of exquisite sensibility," said Ti-Coyo,
going one better. He was throughly enjoying himself.

So loudly did they sing the praises of Uncle
Manidou that the priest expressed a strong desire
to meet him. If this relation really had all the good
qualities the others said he had, he might well
be good for something toward the building of the
chapel. It might even be possible, by dint of a little
persuasion, to decide him to accompany Lucie to
church on Sundays. Anyhow, the attempt was worth
making, and when he learned that Uncle Manidou was temporarily away from home, the good
man uttered his lively regrets. It was the greatest

pity, he said, and he felt really disappointed.

"Uncle Manidou," said Ti-Coyo with an appraising look at the priest's full figure and double chin, "will be even more disappointed."

"As a matter of fact," exclaimed the hunchback, slapping his forehead as though a bright idea had suddenly occurred to him, "I don't see why we shouldn't arrange a meeting . . ."

A gleam of pleasure showed in Guinéo's eyes, and Lucie, who did not at all like the turn the conversation had taken, looked at the hunchback severely.

"You seem to forget," she snapped, "that *Uncle Manidou*" (she deliberately stressed the two words) "has gone off on a journey, and that he hasn't told us when he is likely to be back."

Cocoyo realized that he had gone too far, and hurriedly beat a retreat.

"That's true," he said, though not without a trace of regret in his voice. "I don't know how I came to forget it."

By this time it was getting dark, and the priest was making ready to leave.

Through the open window drifted the gentle sound of the surf lulling the little waves to sleep on the sand at the far end of the path where the shark was dozing in his tank, dreaming of a new tutor

(Guinéo, he knew, would certainly need one) as fat and as tender as his predecessor, and this pleasant prospect set his teeth automatically on end in his mouth.

The tall sugar-canes in the plantation were singing in sheer lightness of heart to the creeping madderwort, which was forever lounging thereabouts. Insects of every kind were enjoying their share of the warmth and sweetness of the rustling dark.

A great peace drooped from the sky, and from the crystal chandelier that hung from the ceiling of the dining-room, and touched the paneling of the walls with gold, and made the glass and heavy silver of the dinner service twinkle against the background made by the spotless cloth.

"May God bless all such families as yours," said the priest with deep feeling as he took his leave.

The hunchback and Ti-Coyo accepted the words with perfect gravity—though they could not help wondering whether the blessing included Uncle Manidou. Guinéo hid his face in Dora's skirt, and Dora squinted happily.

Lucie stole a sidelong glance at him, and was horrified to see that the little wretch's shoulders were shaking with laughter.

A NOTE ON THE TYPE

This book was set on the Linotype in BASKERVILLE, a facsimile of the type designed, in 1754, by John Baskerville, a writing-master of Birmingham, England. This type was one of the forerunners of the "modern" style of type faces. The Linotype copy was cut under the supervision of George W. Jones of London.

Composed, printed, and bound by

H. WOLFF, NEW YORK.